Sno

MW01146963

Sage Gardens Cozy Mystery Series

Cindy Bell

ISBN-13: 978-1542621984

ISBN-10: 1542621984

Table of Contents

Chapter One

"Watch it, Charlie, I almost dropped my tray."

"Sorry June, I'm so clumsy." Charlie made his way to a table not far from Walt's. He settled into the bench seat and heaved a deep sigh. Walt couldn't look away. Charlie also lived in the retirement community, Sage Gardens, and Walt knew that he was only a few years older than him, yet he seemed to have every health issue under the sun, including sight and balance problems. Charlie was a bit of a pet project for Walt, who liked things to be in balance. He'd been doing research into Charlie's multiple conditions in an attempt to find a root cause. He shook his head as he finally looked back across the table at Jo and Eddy.

"Any idea why Samantha wanted us to meet here?" He stirred his tea, then touched the side of his mug. "Tepid. Who wants tepid tea? How can the tea even properly brew?"

"Excuse me?" Jo raised her hand into the air to signal a waitress. "Can we get some boiling water over here please."

"Oh no, it's too late for that. I can't add boiling water to tepid water, it will ruin the tea, which is already half-brewed," Walt said.

Jo shook her head as the waitress walked away. "I guess you have tepid tea then. I'm not sure why she wanted to meet, but she sounded pretty excited."

"I bet it has something to do with that social committee she is on." Eddy took a sip of his coffee. "She's been talking about the trip they're planning all week."

"Oh yes, she asked me to go a few times, but I'm not interested in holing up in some resort with the perky residents of Sage Gardens." Jo laughed. "I'm sure there's a better way I can spend my time."

"I agree." Eddy set his mug down and tilted

2

his head towards the door. "Here she comes."

Samantha pushed through the door and waved to her friends at their usual booth. She adjusted the sleeves of her snowflake-covered sweater, then fluffed the scarf that wrapped around her neck. As she sat down with them, she smiled.

"Samantha, aren't you hot?" Jo tilted her head to the side. "It's at least sixty degrees outside."

"Here, it is." She nodded. "But in Valentine, it's barely over thirty."

"Sounds miserable." Eddy growled. "Better you than me."

"Better all of us." Samantha signaled to the waitress. "Hot chocolate, please." When she looked back at her friends, she couldn't stop smiling. "I made sure there was space on the bus for three more people, even though the three of you neglected to sign up."

"We didn't neglect to sign up, Samantha, we're not going." Jo quirked an eyebrow. "Are you sure all of that warmth isn't making you forgetful."

"I'm not forgetful, you just haven't heard the best part of this retreat."

"What's that?" Walt pushed his tea aside with a sigh.

"It's going to be a murder mystery weekend."

"Great." Eddy laughed. "I've heard of those. Someone pretends to commit a murder, and it's supposed to be fun."

"It isn't the murder part that's fun, Eddy." Samantha rolled her eyes. "It's the solving part!"

"That sounds interesting, Sam, but I'm still not going. I have things to do this weekend," Jo said.

"Like?" Samantha studied her.

"A book to finish, a nap to take, and a bus not to be on."

"Aw, Jo! You're no fun. But I still didn't tell you the best part." She rubbed her hands together.

"Get to it then, I can't stand the anticipation." Walt gazed at her.

"The guests are going to be split up into investigative groups, and there's a prize for the group that solves the murder. A cruise!" She clapped her hands. "I can't wait, I just know we're going to win."

"We?" Eddy shook his head.

"A cruise ship is just a floating petri dish, Samantha. You'll come back with all kinds of intestinal parasites," Walt said.

"Ugh." Samantha took her hot chocolate from the waitress and blew across its surface. "Wow, this is hot."

"Unfair." Walt stared at her mug.

"Anyway, of course if you don't want to go on the cruise you can just sell your ticket. But I do, I've been dreaming about going on a cruise. I just know that we can win. Who could be better at solving crime than us?"

"I don't know," Eddy said.

"Do you know what they have at those resorts?" Walt met her eyes. "Bedbugs. That's what. Bugs that will literally eat you in your sleep."

"Now Walt, they don't eat you," Samantha said.

"In microscopic bites, yes, yes they do." Walt pushed his glasses up and shuddered.

"No way, the committee investigated thoroughly and the resort is guaranteed to be pest free." She patted the back of his hand. "You'll be perfectly safe. I'll make sure of it."

"But that isn't the only concern, Sam. You might get along with the committee crowd, but those women drive me nuts." Eddy narrowed his eyes.

"That's only because you're so handsome. It's not their fault that you're one of the most eligible bachelors. Don't worry, I'll protect you." Samantha smiled.

"Great." Eddy chuckled.

"All right I guess it wouldn't kill us to go," Jo said.

"Nope, the only person getting murdered is the actor playing the victim." Samantha winked. "So, you're all up for it, right? Because I already bought us matching sweaters to wear."

"Matching sweaters?" Jo gasped.

"Relax, I'm joking." Samantha laughed.

"All right, yes, I'll go." Eddy cleared his throat. "Only because I want to exercise my detective skills."

"And I'll go because I'm going to prove that their guarantee is hogwash. Too many people really believe these guarantees that are given to them, and then the bedbugs just keep spreading and spreading. You know there have been a few cases in Sage Gardens. I'm just so relieved that our villas are not connected."

"I didn't know that." Samantha frowned. "What a hassle for whoever dealt with it."

"It is." Walt sighed. "Which is why the truth

must be told."

"Great, so everyone's in?" Samantha looked between her three friends, who all nodded in return. "Then we leave tomorrow morning. It's a three-hour bus trip."

"Can't we just drive?" Eddy frowned. "I'm not sure that I want to be on the bus for that long."

"Don't fuss, Eddy, it'll be fun. I already picked out some songs that we can all sing," Samantha said.

"Sure." Eddy smiled. "I know you better than that, Sam. Singing is not your thing."

"Okay, no songs." She shrugged. "But we'll still have fun. I'm sure of it."

"Listen gentleman, if I'm riding the bus, you are, too." Jo tapped her hand on the table. "We're all in, right?"

"All in." Eddy nodded.

"A bus?" Walt cringed. "Only for Samantha."

"Gee, thanks Walt." She smiled and blew him

a kiss.

Chapter Two

The next morning Samantha woke with a start. Her heart skipped a beat. Had she missed her alarm? One glance at the clock on her bedside table revealed that she was awake twenty minutes early. She was nervous about the trip. Really, she was nervous about the other women on the committee. She had only recently been accepted on to the committee and they were so quick to pick apart her ideas. She knew if things didn't go smoothly they would be ready to pounce. She took a shower to get her head on straight, then grabbed her things and headed to the parking lot.

As Samantha slung her bag over her shoulder, she noticed her friends gathered near the bus. Walt had three bags, one for his laptop, one for his clothes, and one for his cleaning supplies. She could tell because of the bottle of glass cleaning liquid that stuck out of one of the pockets. Jo had a single backpack. She always packed light. Eddy was the only one with a suitcase, old, beat-up, and held together with a bungee cord. It was a small suitcase, but he'd stuffed it pretty full.

"Eddy, what in the world do you have in there?" Samantha smiled as she walked up to the group.

"Books. Lots of books."

"Books? When are you going to have time to read?"

"We'll have the murder mystery solved in twenty minutes. So I'll have the rest of the weekend to avoid interaction with anyone."

"Oh Eddy, where's that good attitude I thought you were going to have?"

"They're all true crime." He shrugged. "Does that help?"

"Yes." She laughed and walked with them over to the bus. Once all of their luggage was stowed, they boarded the bus. It was spacious, but because of the contest incentive, it was packed. They managed to find two benches near the back.

Eddy settled beside the window with Samantha on the outside, and Walt took the window seat in front of them, with Jo on the outside.

Although Samantha was excited for the weekend, and especially for the prize she was certain they would win, when the bus lurched forward, she felt a little uneasy. What if the weekend was horrible? She'd convinced her friends to join her, but she hated to think about them resenting her for it. She decided she would do her best to make it fun, even if they did solve the murder mystery in twenty minutes. About an hour into the bus ride, several of the other people on the bus had begun their third round of traditional bar songs. Eddy thumped his head against the back of the seat, and groaned.

"How did I let you talk me into this?"

"You could always sing along, Eddy." Jo turned around and grinned at him. "Don't act like you don't know the words."

"Maybe I did, at one time, but that was a

different time in my life."

"You mean, it was after half a dozen beers." Samantha smiled.

"That too." Eddy chuckled. "It's much easier to sing nonsense lyrics when you know you won't remember it the next day."

"Don't worry, we have a stop coming up and we'll all get a break." Samantha gritted her teeth. The singing was even getting on her nerves, which took a lot to accomplish. Luckily it began to fade, and gave way to the hum of chatter. She gazed out the window at the scenery that passed. It always made her curious to pass through little towns she'd never been to before. She knew that each was filled with people she would likely never meet. In some ways it made her sad, and in others it gave her inspiration that there might still be adventures left in life.

"Penny for your thoughts?" Eddy patted her knee.

"Oh sorry, just daydreaming." She smiled.

"About?" He met her eyes.

"All the paths not taken I suppose. The ones I've missed, and the ones that are yet to come."

"Interesting perspective. I think about that sometimes, too. It's funny how the plans we make when we are young don't ever seem to lead to the result we expect."

"Ah, but never forget my dear, Eddy, we are still far from the final result. Aren't we?"

"You might be." He grunted. "But I'm getting old."

"I doubt that. One good mystery and you're alive and spunky."

"Spunky?" He chuckled. "I don't think there has ever been a time in my life that I could be described as spunky."

"Trust me, I've seen you get spunky. It's very endearing."

"You're lucky we're friends." He winked at her.

"Yes, yes I am." She smiled and settled back into her daydream. When the bus finally pulled into its first stop, her peaceful state was replaced with horror. The gas station was not what she expected. When planning out the route for the bus trip she'd selected a few places to stop, with the anticipation that everyone on board would want to roam, and have a place to sit and chat before they got back on the bus. Her resource of the gas station must have been out of date, because the multiple picnic tables she expected to find had transformed into one rickety bench, chained to a tree. Though the gas station was still there, when she got off the bus and looked through the window it looked like the store inside was barren of anything that might have been made in the recent years. She was so stunned by the situation that she didn't notice Jo waltz right past her, until she already had the door open.

"Jo, wait. We might just go somewhere else."

"You can go wherever you want, but I have to go right now, I can't wait. I tried the bathroom,

15

but it's locked. The cashier must have a key."

Reluctantly Samantha followed after her. The man behind the counter appeared more faded than the magazine he flipped through. His skin was dry, his lips cracked, and his clothes were smudged with dust and dirt. Samantha couldn't imagine what he did to get into such a state. Did he roll around in the dirt between customers? She reminded herself it was not right to judge, and requested the bathroom key.

"Nah, it's not locked, you just have to kick it, then slam your hip into it, it'll open." He smiled, a nearly toothless smile. Samantha smiled back at him, then steered Jo out of the store.

"Can you believe this?"

"It's not too unusual for an out of the way place. You can't expect five stars on a road trip." Jo did as the cashier instructed and kicked the door, then slammed it with her hip. The door popped open, and a horrid odor seeped out. "Wow, I stand corrected, this place is what I call roughing it." Jo scrunched up her nose at the smell of the bathroom. "And I've been in some pretty rough situations."

"I know, it's already a disaster, isn't it? How am I going to explain any of this to the rest of the group? I promised a fun weekend, and so far all I've delivered is a rundown gas station with a bathroom that should be quarantined."

"Relax. Just take a breath. On second thought, don't." Jo pinched her nose and stepped into the bathroom. "What I'm trying to say is that the weekend has just begun. So there's a bump in the road, that's bound to happen. Everything will be fine once we get to the resort. All of this will just be a memory."

"I hope so. I'm never going to live it down with the committee."

"Don't worry about those gals, if they want to torment you over something as petty as this, then they're not exactly the type of people you want around you anyway. Are they?"

"No, I guess not." Samantha shrugged. "Thanks Jo."

"You're welcome. Now, let's get out of here, I think I'd rather go in the woods."

"Jo!"

"I'm just kidding. But you might want to warn Walt to hold it in until the next stop."

"Yes, you're right. I should." Samantha shuddered at the idea of Walt walking into such a filthy bathroom. When she stepped outside she noticed three of the committee members huddled near the bus. She knew that couldn't mean anything good. As she rounded the corner she walked right into Eddy.

"Oops, excuse me, Sam."

"No, it's okay, I'm the one that wasn't looking. Have you seen Walt?"

"He refuses to leave the bus. He's certain there's tetanus in the dirt that can be kicked up into the air and breathed in."

"Is that even possible?" Samantha lifted an eyebrow.

"I doubt it, but he's in panic mode, so it's best not to argue."

"I bet you're already wishing you'd stayed home, instead of agreeing to this trip."

"Sure I am." He smiled.

"Ugh, thanks a lot, Eddy."

"Look, I make no secret of the fact that I'd rather be at home in my comfortable chair, but that's not because of anything you did. That's just what I would prefer. You have my support, as always."

"I'm glad, because I have a feeling I'm going to need it."

As she walked towards the bus, the three women set their sights on her. She could sense their disapproval in their seething expressions.

"Samantha, we need to talk." Amber fluffed her hair, then looked into her eyes. "This, is a disaster."

"It's just one bad stop, ladies. I'm sure the next one will be much better," Samantha said.

"Oh? Because I'm not sure at all." Stephanie crossed her arms. "In fact I'm almost certain that the next stop is going to be worse than this one. To be honest, the only thing stopping me from calling a cab right now, is knowing that we're going to win that cruise."

"I'm sorry that you're not having a good time, but I think if you try to relax a little and open your mind, you will have a much better experience." Samantha looked between them. "You're that confident that you'll win?"

"Sure. Who's our competition?" Amber looked past Samantha, to where Jo and Eddy stood watching. "Your little group of wanna-be detectives?"

"I think we stand a fair chance."

"You're wrong. My friends and I will have this murder mystery solved in just a few minutes, and then we get to start planning our cruise. Right ladies?"

The other two women nodded their agreement, then all three boarded the bus. Samantha did her best to hold her tongue, but the person standing behind her did not do the same.

"I thought I heard some cackling." Eddy smirked.

"Eddy, they're right, this is a disaster."

"It's not that bad, Sam." Jo walked up with a smile.

"I'm sorry guys. I'll understand if you want to find a way back from here. You don't have to stick out this awful trip with me. It was wrong of me to ask you to come in the first place."

"No way." Eddy narrowed his eyes. "I'm not going anywhere but back on that bus."

"Really?" Samantha stared at him.

"Sure, someone's going to have to show them just how a crime is solved. Those three old bats aren't going on a cruise anytime soon."

"Eddy, all three of them are probably younger than you."

"So?" He scowled. "That doesn't change the fact that they're bats. They just want to cause trouble. I'm not going to put up with that. Are you, Jo?"

"No. I'm not. I want to solve the murder, too. You can't let women like that push you around, Sam. You have to show them what you're made of, or they'll just keep pushing."

"Wow, you two are amazing. I really appreciate the support. You're right, Jo, I should stand up to them, but first I want to win the cruise. But what about Walt?"

"Walt's got his own mystery to solve. He wants to prove that there are bedbugs at the resort. I doubt that anyone could get him to change his mind at this point. He is one determined fellow."

"All right, then let's go. The sooner we get

there, the sooner we win."

"And the sooner we can pee safely." Jo laughed and led Samantha onto the bus. Once everyone was settled, the bus lurched forward. The next two stops went smoothly, but with each stop they made, the temperature in the air around them dropped. Everyone on the bus began layering with sweaters and jackets. The roads became steeper as the bus rolled up into the mountains. Samantha smiled as she stared out the window.

"I think we're definitely going to see some snow."

"I hope so." Jo grinned. "A little bit is always nice."

"Look!" Samantha pointed through the window. "I saw a snowflake! It's snowing everyone!"

A cheer rippled through the bus followed by a lot of chatter. Samantha gazed at the snowflakes as they fluttered down around the bus. It was soothing to watch. However, by the time the bus drew close to the resort, the snowflakes no longer fluttered. They streamed down, aided by a forceful wind. The bitter air squeezed through the windows of the bus and even with the heat on high, everyone began to complain of the cold. Samantha held her tongue and hoped that they would arrive before everyone got too cranky. The bus drove slower, and slower.

"Sorry folks, have to be cautious on these slippery roads." The driver called back over his shoulder. Samantha was glad he was being cautious, but it seemed as if they would never arrive and get off the bus.

Chapter Three

When the resort finally loomed ahead of them, Samantha was impressed by how modern it looked, with many glass windows, and splashes of color throughout. Everyone forgot about how cold they were, and buzzed with excitement instead. Even Eddy smiled as he pointed out the rambling four story building that they approached.

"Wow, this is a fancy place."

"It is fancy." Samantha smiled and clapped her hands, more to keep them warm than to express excitement. "I'm glad we made it."

"Me too." Walt shifted in his seat. "I think I'm going to need to see a chiropractor before I'm able to regain my posture."

"Trust me, Walt, a night or two in these cozy beds and you're going to be walking tall." Samantha pointed to the brochure in her hand. "Feathertop mattresses, all around."

"Cozy beds, full of bedbugs," Walt mumbled as he followed them off the bus.

Once everyone was organized with their room cards and the plan to meet for dinner, Samantha breathed a sigh of relief.

"Well, we made it here, I guess that's half the battle." She glanced out the window. "Oh, and look, it's snowing." She smiled. "Even harder than it was on the way here."

"Wonderful." Eddy patted his belly. "Now, where's the bar?" He grinned.

"Just down there next to the dining hall. Listen, take this." She pressed a ticket into his hand. "It'll get you a few free drinks."

"Thanks, I wonder what it includes?"

"Just ask the bartender."

"I will. See you ladies at dinner."

"Don't you want to check out our room first?" Walt frowned.

"Walt buddy, I wouldn't want to get in the way

of your fumigating."

"Good point." Walt nodded. "It's best if I assess the situation first."

"I'll take your suitcase up." Jo grabbed the handle, then grunted. "You really did pack a lot of books, didn't you?"

"And rocks, just a few rocks." Eddy waved as he walked off towards the bar.

In the elevator, Walt surveyed the structure around them. "Up to date, and fitted with the latest emergency equipment. At least the elevator is in good condition."

"I think everything here will meet your standards, Walt. This resort got great reviews." Samantha watched as Jo let go of Eddy's heavy suitcase. It thumped to the floor.

"Easy, no sudden movements." Walt frowned. "You know, Samantha, some of those reviews are paid for. You never can tell whether someone is being honest or not."

"True, but there weren't any bad ones. I

27

imagine if anyone had a bad experience they would have reported it."

"Fair enough." Walt nodded. The elevator doors slid open and they stepped off into the second floor hallway.

"Walt, you and Eddy have room 207, and Jo and I are next door in 209." She handed him a key card.

"Oh good, not far from the elevator." Walt smiled his approval and unlocked the door. Jo heaved the suitcase inside.

"Oh no, don't put it on the floor!" Walt gasped. "The suitcases have to go in the bathtub until the room is cleared of bedbugs, otherwise we'll be bringing them home with us. Just go, please, I can handle it from here."

"Okay, okay." Jo met his eyes. "If you need anything just let us know."

"All right, I will." He began to unload his cleaning supplies. Samantha and Jo walked to the next door, unlocked it and stepped inside.

28

"You weren't kidding, Sam, I'm glad I came. This room is gorgeous."

"Isn't the décor wonderful? The decorator adds in all of these little gems." She touched the flower petal painted on the wall beside one of the light switches. "I think they take away from the coldness of a hotel room."

"Yes, they do. And oh look!" Jo grinned as she opened one of the cabinets. "Fresh tea leaves! Most places leave only tea bags. It's refreshing to see that tea leaves is an option, too."

"You should make yourself a cup. I'm going to get unpacked and settled. I want some time away from the group before dinner tonight. Those three ladies are going to be on the warpath and I'd rather not butt heads."

"Just remember, don't let them..."

"I know, I know, don't let them push me around. It's hard not to. I'm trying to be friendly with them, but they are just so set in their ways."

"Why are you trying to be friendly with

them?"

"Because I like organizing things. It has taken me so long to be accepted on to the committee and I like being part of the group that puts on all of the entertainment. It's exciting. It keeps me busy."

"Ah, retirement isn't working so well for you is it?"

"It is, and it isn't. I do feel like I need something to do all of the time. Before I retired I looked forward to having less responsibilities and more free time. But now, I have no idea what to do with it. So it's nice to have some kind of plan for the year. I know when the parties will be, when we have to start getting ready for them, approximately how many people will be included in them. That's all stuff that can keep me on my toes."

"I understand. That's why I enjoy my garden so much. I participate in a certain cycle. I know when things need to be planted, when they need to be watered, when they need to be harvested.

That all makes a big difference in my daily life. I guess, not having some kind of routine or schedule to follow can make anyone feel unhinged."

"Anyone but Eddy." Samantha shook her head. "He seems to handle things just fine."

"Does he? That's because he hasn't retired."

"What do you mean? He's as retired as the rest of us."

"He may claim he is, but all of those true crime books are just a way to hone his skills. He's constantly solving cases, whether he gets paid for it or not. Haven't you ever noticed the way he's always got his eye on someone or something? He never just sits back and closes his eyes, or looks at the scenery."

"You're right. I hadn't noticed that. Probably because I was too busy looking at the scenery."

"He's just a very alert guy. I hope one day he learns how to relax a little though, because he's missing out on fun."

31

"Well, maybe his trip to the bar will help with that." Samantha stretched. "I say we unpack and then head down to join him."

"Sounds good. Should I put my suitcase in the bathtub?"

"Only if you plan on soaking it." Samantha grinned. "Don't worry, this place is spotless!"

"Hm." Jo glanced around the room again. It was quite beautiful, but she knew better than to be fooled by the appearance of things.

Chapter Four

Eddy was relieved to find that the bar was not very populated with people from the bus yet. Most had likely gone to settle in their rooms and prepare for dinner. Since there were free welcome drinks he was sure they soon would be arriving in droves. However, for the moment, there were only a handful of other people in the bar. He settled on one of the stools at the bar, and nodded to the bartender. If he saw Eddy's nod, he showed no sign of it, as his focus was elsewhere. There was a table with a small group of men and women, dressed in rather strange clothes. It appeared to Eddy that the clothes were dated, as if they came straight out of the twenties. A ripple of laughter rose up from the table, and the bartender shook his head. Only then did he notice Eddy.

"Hi there, what can I get for you?"

"Beer please." Eddy held up the voucher Samantha had given him.

"Sure. In the bottle?"

"Yes please." One thing that being friends with Walt had taught him, was never to trust the glasses at a bar. They often were not cleaned properly. The bartender handed him an ice-cold beer. "What's the deal with that group?" Eddy tilted his head towards the strangely dressed people.

"Oh, those are the actors. They put on the murder mystery. They've just finished their dress rehearsal for tomorrow."

"Oh, how nice." Eddy took a sip of his beer and looked over at the group again. "Which one is getting offed?"

"You know I can't tell you that." The bartender grinned. "I wouldn't want to ruin the surprise."

"All right, fair enough." Eddy sipped his beer as the bar began to fill up.

One of the men at the table with the other actors stood up and walked up to the end of the bar.

"Excuse me." The bartender walked over to serve the man. "A free beer? You know they're on the house for all of the actors."

"No thanks. Just a water please. Is that on the house, too? I guess it's better than being on the floor." He chuckled at his own joke. Eddy looked back towards the group of people. There was a time when his only friends were police officers. After retiring it took him some time to make friends with people that weren't in law enforcement. Now that he had a small but tight knit group around him, that sense of security that someone always had his back, had returned to his life. As the actor rejoined the others, Eddy finished his beer and continued to observe the people around him. It was in his nature to blend into the background while constantly keeping an eye on everyone else.

For Eddy's second drink he ordered a soda, and kept his attention on the door. He thought perhaps Jo, or Samantha would wander in, but when neither did he decided to head for the dining hall. As he stood up he put a few folded bills on the bar.

"Oh, no need for a tip, the drinks were complimentary."

"There's always need for a tip." Eddy winked at him.

"In that case, don't be afraid to ask for me. Ben." He held out his hand to Eddy. Eddy gave it a quick shake.

"Eddy."

"Are you here for the murder mystery?"

"Yes, in fact, my friends and I will likely be the ones to solve it."

"Confident, huh?" Ben chuckled.

"I'm a retired police detective, if I can't figure out a fake murder, who can?"

"Good point." He cleared his throat. "Good luck to you and your friends."

"Thanks."

Eddy made his way through the crowd to the door of the bar. As he headed in the direction of the dining hall, he spotted Walt, Samantha, and Jo coming from the opposite direction.

"If you're going to the bar, don't bother. It's getting way too crowded in there."

"No, going to dinner. I reserved a table for the four of us." Samantha smiled.

"Oh good. I'm starving."

"Do you think I could speak to the chef first?" Walt scrunched up his nose. "I'd like to know how he checks the temperature of his meat."

"I think the chef might be a little too busy for that, Walt." Samantha pointed out the crowded dining room. "Not only is our group here, but there are some others staying here as well. Only our group is taking part in the murder mystery though."

"Good, I can't wait to get it solved so I can settle in with some books." Eddy held the door for Samantha, Jo, and Walt so that Walt wouldn't have to touch the knob. Once they were seated the dining hall began to fill up even more. The wait staff rushed around providing drink orders and taking orders.

"I really do think this is a nice place." Jo sat back in her chair. "Even though it's crowded, I haven't heard one cross word from any of the staff. Everyone is friendly."

"Oh, I got a preview of the actors who will put on the murder mystery tomorrow. They were in the bar," Eddy said.

"How exciting." Samantha leaned forward. "Do you know who the murderer is?"

"No, I asked the bartender who the victim was and he said he couldn't tell me."

"Well, that's good, we don't want to spoil the fun anyway."

"I hope it's at least a little challenging." Jo glanced over her shoulder, then lowered her voice. "Maybe I'll get to use some of my special skills." Eddy cringed slightly at the reference to

Jo's past career as a cat burglar.

"I think we're all going to get to use some of our special skills. I've heard about this group, and they put on a fantastic mystery. Some people don't figure it out at all, until the reveal." Samantha smiled at the waitress as she brought their food. Once she was gone, Walt used a fork to inspect his food.

"Well, I can tell you, I want the chance to show the housekeeping staff here how to actually clean a bathroom. Our room is very nice, but the bathroom has been neglected."

"Is there any bathroom clean enough for you, Walt?" Eddy met his eyes.

"Not even my own, I'm afraid." Walt sighed. As Samantha took the last bite of her meal she heard a commotion near the front of the dining hall. When she looked in that direction she caught sight of a man in an old-fashioned suit, and another man. They appeared to be arguing, but she couldn't hear exactly what they said.

"Well, that was delicious." Eddy patted his stomach. "But I'm stuffed."

"Are you going up to your room? Jo and I were going to use our free drink tickets in the bar."

"I used mine already. I'd rather have a nap."

"Okay, but if you change your mind, come and join us." Samantha looked across the table at Walt. "Are you going to join us?"

"Absolutely. I want to check the temperature of their beer. Did you know that sour beer can lead to at least ten different kinds of health problems?"

"Walt!" Jo laughed.

"It's true. You'll appreciate it."

"I'm sure we will." Samantha grinned at him. Eddy waved to them, then left the dining hall. The moment he was gone, Samantha frowned. "I don't think he's going to have any fun while he's here. I feel guilty for convincing him to come along."

"Oh, don't let that tough attitude fool you." Jo finished the last of her drink. "He's happy to be here. He just can't let you see it. What else would he be doing back at Sage Gardens?"

"That's true. Just about anything he could do there, he can do here, too."

"Exactly." Jo smiled.

The three left the dining hall and entered the bar through a door that shared a wall with the dining hall. Once inside, the noise level raised considerably.

"Wow, it's crowded in here." Samantha lingered close to Jo.

"Not my kind of crowd." Jo frowned. "Maybe we should skip the free drinks."

"But they're free." Walt pushed his glasses up and looked between the two of them. "Do you know how few things are free in life?"

"I guess he has a point." Jo squinted. "I think I see some open stools over there at the end of the bar."

"Let's try to get them before someone else

does." Samantha cut right through the crowd while Walt and Jo picked their way through. Once they reached the bar stools, Walt whipped out a wipe and cleaned off the seat and the bar in front of him. "Want me to do yours?" He looked over at Jo.

"No thanks, I'll risk it." She smiled as she settled on the stool beside him.

"Just a second, I'll be right with you." A young man rushed past them to the other end of the bar.

"Poor guy is getting overworked tonight." Jo skimmed the people around them. "I recognize a lot of these people, but there are many faces I don't. I wonder why it's so crowded?"

"When I got the tickets for the murder mystery, the rooms were dirt cheap. I guess in the winter season they sell the rooms for cheaper."

"I wonder why that is?"

"I think I may have an idea." Walt held up his phone. "I just received a weather alert."

"For what?" Samantha peered at his phone.

"A blizzard." Walt lowered his phone and met her eyes. "Did you know anything about this?"

"No, of course not. I didn't even look at the weather really. I figured it was too early for any big snows."

"Not here it isn't. Blizzards are common this time of year."

"Oh no." She groaned. "If we get snowed in, I'll never hear the end of it."

"I'm sure it'll pass. Right Walt? What does the warning say exactly?" Jo asked.

"It says, warning, you're about to be snowed in." He stared at them both.

"What? Really?" Samantha peered at his phone again.

"No not really, but that was funny, wasn't it?" He grinned.

"Oh, Walt told a joke!" Jo clapped her hands and winked at him. "Sounds to me like you're really starting to relax and enjoy yourself."

"Yes, actually I am." Walt nodded. "But the warning is pretty direct. There's not much chance that the snow storm is going to miss us."

"Oh well." Jo shrugged. "We were going to spend the weekend inside anyway. We can make the best of it. Try not to worry, Sam."

"Thanks Jo." Samantha stared down at her own phone as the weather report paraded past. The massive blob that represented snow was headed straight for the resort.

"Put that away, let's have our drinks, and have some fun." Jo tapped the top of Samantha's phone.

"All right, I will." Samantha tucked her phone into her purse and tried not to think about the storm that was coming. There was nothing that could be done about it now.

The music shifted from peppy, to wild. Samantha noticed a large group from Sage Gardens having a good time as they clustered around tables in the bar. At least things were going well so far. Suddenly, a spotlight shone on a group of people near the back wall of the bar.

"Ladies and gentlemen, a round of applause for our talented actors who will be hosting a one of a kind murder mystery tomorrow." The people at the table all stood up as everyone applauded. Each person was dressed in old-fashioned clothing, and the women had updos that hovered a few inches above their heads. It was clear that the actors took their jobs seriously. Samantha started to get excited about the mystery the next day.

"I think this is really going to be interesting."

"Oh?" The bartender leaned against the bar. "It might be more interesting if you let me make you our specialty drink."

"No, that's all right, I don't like fancy drinks."

"Who said it was fancy?" He laughed. "Just special."

"Well, all right, I guess I could try it. Thanks."

"Would you like one as well?" He looked at Jo.

45

"No thanks."

"One specialty drink coming up." He turned away from them and grabbed a glass. When he turned back he began flipping bottles of alcohol in different directions. Samantha cheered as he tossed one bottle under one arm, and the other under the other. Then he managed to catch them both. Walt cried out and shook his head.

"That's so reckless!"

"It's amazing." Samantha grinned. "You're very talented."

"Thank you." He offered a small bow, then topped off her drink with a pink, plastic flower. "Something special, for someone special." He handed her the glass.

"Wow." She ducked her head and hoped that he didn't notice the flush in her cheeks. As she took a sip of the drink, she smiled even wider.

"Yum, this is very interesting."

"You're right." The bartender smiled at her. "It's about to get even more interesting." He winked, then walked away.

"What do you think that means?" Samantha glanced at her friends.

"Either he's coming back to ask for your number, or..." The light in the bar suddenly dimmed. A disco light lowered from the ceiling as a few staff members cleared some tables out of the way. "Or that." Jo laughed.

"Flickering lights are responsible for seventy-five percent of seizures, did you know that?" Walt shook his head.

"You just made that up because you don't want to dance, didn't you?" Samantha raised an eyebrow.

"Maybe." Walt squinted through the dim light. "It would be nice if I could order another water, but the staff seem to be occupied. I think I'll head back to the room."

"Wait for us, we'll walk up with you." Jo grabbed her purse. "Unless you want to dance, Sam?"

"No way, I want to be well rested for the murder mystery tomorrow." As the trio began to make their way through the crowd, Samantha noticed that there were a lot of people dancing. All of the smiles and laughter indicated that so far, the weekend was off to a great start.

Chapter Five

The room was spotless, thanks to Walt, and it was also very comfortable. There were several little touches that made Eddy feel as if he was home, especially the recliner. It wasn't as soft and broken-in as his recliner back home, but he sunk into it fairly well. As Eddy began to relax, he flipped on the television and settled back in the chair. His peace was disrupted seconds later when a shrill sound carried through the speakers on the television. A dark red bar ran across the bottom of the screen, detailing a severe weather warning.

"Oh, that's not good." Eddy frowned as he watched the weather radar on the television. He reached for his phone to text Samantha about the incoming storm, but discovered it was dead. He searched the room for his phone charger, but he couldn't find it anywhere. Frustrated, he decided to just head down to the bar to talk to Samantha in person. As he left the room he noticed that the hallways were empty. In fact the entire resort was quiet. He could only guess that just about everyone was in the bar. That guess was proven to be true when he reached the dining hall and discovered that there wasn't a single person in it. It had been tidied up and all of the chairs were pushed under the tables. As he rounded one of the tables to head for the bar, his foot caught on something. He looked down, puzzled, to see a shoe.

"Who would leave a shoe behind?" He started to walk past, then realized there was more than a shoe. The shoe was attached to a body, half-hidden by a tablecloth. His heart raced as he saw something sharp and long sticking out of the chest of the man on the floor. He reached for his phone, then remembered that he didn't have it on him.

"Help!" He crouched down to check the man's pulse, and found that his skin was warm. But he didn't feel anything against his fingertips. "Help!" He jumped up when he realized there was no one around to hear him. He ran to the bar and shoved the door open. Going from the bright light of the dining hall to the dim and flickering lights of the bar, made him dizzy for a second.

"Help!" He shouted as loud as he could, but the music drowned out the sound of his voice. He grabbed a woman near the entrance. "I need you to call an ambulance, someone has been stabbed."

"What are you talking about?" She pulled free of his grasp. "Don't touch me! Are you drunk?"

"Someone's been stabbed, please call an ambulance," Eddy said when he spotted Amber walking past him.

"Stabbed?" Amber asked skeptically.

"Yes. Please call an ambulance!" Eddy said with urgency.

"I don't have my phone, but I'll go tell security," Amber said as she pushed through the crowd as she walked away from Eddy.

"Samantha!" Eddy shoved through the crowd towards the bar. "Jo!"

"Is that Eddy?" Samantha strained to see around the people in front of her. "Eddy?"

"Sam, call 911, there's a body in the dining hall."

"A body?"

"Someone's been stabbed! Do you have your phone?"

"Yes, I do, hold on." Just as Samantha pulled it out, the lights in the bar turned back on and the music stopped. A ripple of shrieks carried through the crowd in reaction to the sudden change.

"Everyone calm down please, calm down!" Ben stood on top of the bar. "There's been a report of a crime. If you could all please exit the bar through the side doors in an orderly fashion we can get this sorted out."

Security staff began to pour in from the opposite door. A man with a badge on his suit jacket walked up to Eddy.

"My name is Bart, I'm head of security here. Are you the one that reported finding a body?"

"He's in the dining hall." Eddy gestured towards the dining hall. "On the floor, by one of the tables."

"The dining hall? Are you sure about that, sir?" Bart looked into Eddy's eyes.

"Yes, I'm certain. He was on the floor, with something sticking out of his chest."

"Sir, we just came through the dining hall, there was no one there."

"You must have missed him. I almost did, too. Here, I'll show you." Eddy stepped back through the door with his friends right behind him. The security guard surveyed the dining hall as Eddy walked through it. He stared with disbelief at the empty floor. He walked between each table, and then shook his head.

"Someone must have moved the body. He was right there. I saw him. I even checked for a pulse."

"Sir, perhaps you were confused. Can you give me a description of the man that you saw?"

"He was uh, in his fifties I think. He had short

brown hair. Oh, and he was wearing one of those old-fashioned suits."

"Old-fashioned suits?"

"Yes, like the actors that were in the bar earlier."

"Oh. Like a costume?" The security guard cleared his throat.

"I don't know if it was a costume or not, but that was what he was wearing." Eddy growled. "Are you going to shut this place down and do a thorough search or do I need to call in the FBI?"

"Eddy." Samantha rested her hand on his elbow. "I'm sure he's doing everything he should be."

"It's possible that the man you saw was one of the actors in the murder mystery. Sometimes they practice their role before the opening act." The security guard pulled out his radio. "Stand down, there's no body."

"There most certainly is a body! You just have to find it, that's your job isn't it?" Eddy asked.

"Sir, I'm sorry, but it's clear that you were mistaken. Perhaps you had a little too much to drink?"

"I did not!" Eddy's voice raised so loud, that Walt took a step back, and Jo put her hand on Eddy's other arm.

"Settle down, Eddy, we'll figure this out. Obviously, there's been some kind of mistake. Maybe it was just an act," Jo said.

"Oh, is there some kind of new acting trick that can keep a person from having a pulse?" Eddy gently pushed off both Samantha and Jo's hands as he approached the security guard. "Now you listen to me! Every second that passes is an opportunity for someone to get away with murder. You need to get your men to conduct a thorough search of this entire resort. If you can't handle that, then you should call in law enforcement, who can. If you won't, I will. Samantha, give me your phone!" He turned back to face Samantha, who handed over her phone without argument. Eddy's flushed cheeks and sharp tone warned all of his friends that he was not to be silenced.

"I'm afraid that will not be possible, sir." The security guard crossed his arms.

"Excuse me? You can't stop me from reporting a crime."

"No, sir, I can't. But there is no way law enforcement is going to be able to come out here at this time. All of the roads leading to the resort have already been closed due to the heavy snowfall."

"Oh no." Eddy groaned. "I forgot about the storm. That was the whole reason I came down to the bar."

"It's very important to us that you feel safe here, Eddy." The security guard offered his hand. "I'm sure if we work together we can figure out what happened here. If you give me some time, I will ensure there is a search of the grounds, and I will also make contact with the actor that I think you might have seen. Everything will be fine."

"Unless you're planning to break out some kind of séance you're not going to be making any contact with the man that I saw dead on this floor."

"Eddy, he's just trying to be helpful. Try to think this through. If there was a body here..."

"If? If Samantha?" He stared straight into her eyes. "Are you saying that I didn't see what I know I saw?"

"I'm not saying that at all." Samantha looked him straight back in the eyes. "I'm telling you that you need to calm down if we're going to figure this out."

"You're right." He heaved a deep sigh and nodded. "I'm sorry. Obviously, something strange has happened here. I know what I saw, but the body is gone. So someone must have moved it."

"I will have my security team scour the grounds, but in the meantime, it would be best if you returned to your rooms."

"All right." Eddy frowned and joined his

57

friends as they walked towards the hallway that led to the rooms. His heart raced as he knew that every second that passed was a second longer for the killer to escape. "I can't believe they're being so casual about this. Someone has to find the killer."

"And they will, Eddy." Samantha pushed the button to call the elevator. "But we have to let them do their job."

"Why? So they can cover up a murder on their property? That's all they want to do. It'll be bad for sales if someone was killed in their resort," Eddy said.

The elevator doors slid shut.

"Eddy has a point, it does cause a huge problem if there is a murder in a luxury resort," Walt said.

"Still, I doubt that the security staff would go to the lengths of moving a body in order to protect the resort. That would mean they could all be going to prison for their interference," Samantha said.

When they reached the second floor Samantha held the doors open until all of her friends walked through.

The four friends stepped into Walt and Eddy's room and closed the door behind them. "Moving the body is too big of a risk to take, for anyone." Walt shook his head.

"Depending on how much they're paid." Jo shrugged. "Maybe the payoff is worth the risk."

"I don't know, this is a nice place, but it's not exactly the playground of billionaires. I really don't think that the staff moved the body." Samantha shook her head.

"If there was a body, where did it go?" Walt sat down at the table and took off his glasses to clean them.

"If? I don't see why we're even debating this, I know what I saw. All of you are acting like I didn't see what I saw, but I know what I saw." Eddy looked between his three friends in search of an explanation.

"I don't know what you expect us to say, Eddy. You say there was a body, but there isn't one. There's no blood, no sign of a crime being committed. So how can there be a murder with no evidence? Not even a body?" Jo asked.

"I saw one, that's how. I'm not sure how you can question it."

"It's not that we're questioning you, Eddy, we're looking for the logical explanation." Walt wiped his glasses clean, then placed them back on his face. "Of course you saw what you saw, no one is doubting that."

"Really? Because it seems like all of you are."

"You're just wound up, Eddy. You know us better than that. If you think we're not going to support you then you've really lost touch with reality." Jo patted his shoulder. "But the point is, what you saw is now gone. So, we are going to have to figure out why that is, and where it might be. Maybe if you go over exactly what you saw one more time, we could piece something together."

"But first have some tea." Walt walked over with a cup. "Just drink it, and sit down for a few minutes. The security team is running a search of the resort and the grounds. There's nothing else we can do, other than to try to think this through."

"Thanks, Walt. You're right. I'm sorry for barking at you guys. I just got so upset when that security idiot acted like I was seeing things. Over twenty years with a badge, but I'm making things up?"

"Nobody thinks that, Eddy." Samantha sat down beside him at the table. "Just try to calm your nerves a little bit."

"No one here believes you're making anything up." Jo sat down across from him. "None of us doubt what you saw. But keep in mind, sometimes what we see can be an illusion."

"So you think it was some kind of prank that I fell for?"

"Stop taking things so personally, Eddy. It's

not about you. It's about the victim, isn't it?" Jo asked.

"The imaginary one?" Eddy shook his head.

"Jo's right, Eddy. You need to calm down and think this through. No matter what, something strange has happened here, and we're the only ones that believe it," Samantha said.

"Okay, okay. I'll try my best to keep things straight in my mind. I'll admit, I'm pretty wound up about this. I don't like to be treated that way."

"No one does, but no one is immune to it either. Why don't you tell me again, exactly what you saw?" Jo met his eyes.

"I saw a man on the floor with something sticking out of his chest."

"Something?"

"I can't say exactly what it was. It was some kind of tool."

"But you're sure it was in his chest?"

"Yes, of course I am. Then I checked for a

pulse. His skin was still warm, but there was no pulse. So he'd just been killed."

"Or maybe you just felt in the wrong place?" Samantha sat down on the other side of him.

"Samantha!"

"Eddy." She put her hand on his. "We all make mistakes sometimes. Not every human being is designed the same. Maybe this man has some kind of defect which makes it hard to feel his pulse in his neck. Did you check his wrist?"

"No, I didn't." He frowned. "I didn't have my phone. I wanted to get help as fast as I could."

"That's totally understandable. Do you think it's possible he was alive?"

"No." Eddy's lips drew into a straight, thin line. "I saw his chest, I saw the body, I know he was dead."

"All right, then we can all agree to that."

"You can?"

"Yes." Samantha looked at the others. "Can't

we?"

"Yes, if you say so, Eddy, I believe you." Jo nodded.

"Yes, I agree as well. However, I want to also point out, that dead bodies don't just disappear, so we need to get to the bottom of this," Walt said.

"I agree." Eddy sighed. "If it wasn't the security staff, then maybe." He paused.

"What is it, Eddy?" Samantha prompted him.

"Maybe I interrupted the murder by arriving when I did. Maybe the killer was hiding somewhere in the dining hall. When I ran to get help, maybe the killer moved the body. It's the only time that it could have been done."

"And if the killer moved the body, it had to be done fast. So that limits the options," Walt said.

"But now that we've wasted time waiting for the security staff to believe me, there's a good chance the killer has found another way to hide the body."

"Good point. The body might have been hidden temporarily, and then moved again." Walt cleared his throat.

"So, not only do we have a body floating around here somewhere, we have a desperate murderer as well, who may consider Eddy the only witness to his crime." Jo looked across the table at him. "You need to keep that in mind. Your safety could be at risk."

As if to punctuate her words, there was a loud knock on the door. Walt jumped. Samantha stood up and walked over to the door. Eddy followed after her. When she answered it, the head of security greeted both of them.

"I thought you might want an update. Our security team just finished the search, and there is no sign of any body anywhere on the property. Of course the grounds are inaccessible because of the storm. We have yet to reach Howard, the actor we think you saw, but that's not surprising. He's a bit of a drunk, and he is probably off somewhere sleeping it off. Listen, he probably got liquored up and decided to pull a prank, I'm sorry that you were the butt of it."

"There's no way it was a prank. You're really not going to do another search?" Eddy asked.

"I don't have anything to look for. Maybe in the morning, we'll take another look around. But I'm sure by then we'll have found Howard, and we can put all of this to rest. For tonight, just try to relax, and trust me when I tell you, what you think you saw, wasn't actually a murder victim."

"Sure." Eddy crossed his arms. "Thanks for your efforts."

"If you have any more concerns please don't hesitate to call the front desk. We have staff available all night."

"Great. If I need a cup of warm milk, I'll be sure to ring."

"All right, sir." He nodded, then turned and walked out of the room.

"Eddy, you didn't have to be so brusque, he's only doing his job." Samantha closed the door behind him.

"I know, I know, I'm the bad guy here. But are you forgetting that someone is dead, and no one is trying to figure out why, or who did it?" Eddy shook his head. "That doesn't seem like something that I should be nice about. If it seems like that to you, then it's not my attitude that you should be worried about."

"You don't need to attack me," Samantha said.

"I'm not attacking you." He groaned with frustration.

"Enough. Eddy is right. If there was a murder we can't just pretend there wasn't. We have to figure out what happened to the body. The security staff isn't taking this seriously. I say we do our own search," Jo said.

"How are we going to do that? There's three foot of snow outside," Walt said.

"And the snow was already falling when Eddy saw the body." Samantha snapped her fingers.

"Which means that whoever moved the body wouldn't be able to get it off the property. So, it more than likely has to be hidden here somewhere inside of the resort."

"If we do a floor by floor search we might be able to find something. Most of the guests will already be in their rooms for the night so it should be easy to accomplish. If I can look up the floor plans of the resort, then we can split up and each take a section to search." Walt pulled out his laptop and began to search for the plans.

"Always prepared." Samantha smiled.

"That's a great idea, Walt. Let's do it." Jo paced through the center of the room.

"There's four of us, and four floors, but one of the floors has a separate wing with the kitchen, bar and dining hall. It is on the ground floor and it also has some rooms for the staff as well as the lobby, recreation room and café in the main wing."

"I should take the separate wing on the

ground floor as it is probably locked up for the night," Jo said.

"You're going to break in?" Samantha frowned. "What if we get caught? We might get kicked out."

"Do you really think they're going to throw us out in the snow?" Jo shook her head. "That wouldn't exactly be good business. Can you picture the headline? Guests found frozen after getting the cold shoulder."

"Good point."

"So, it's a plan then?" Eddy glanced between the group.

"Yes." Walt nodded. "Eddy, which floor would you like?" Walt showed him the floor plans on his computer. "The first floor has eighteen rooms and four supply closets. The second floor has fifteen rooms and the gym and only two supply closets, and the third floor has fifteen rooms, two supply closets, and the stairs that lead to the roof."

"I'll take the first and third floors. It's possible

that the murderer decided to hide the body in one of the supply closets, or even on the roof," Eddy said.

"I think I should take the rest of the ground floor, so Jo can concentrate on the dining wing," Walt said.

"Good idea." Eddy nodded.

"Okay, that leaves you the second floor, Samantha. Does that sound okay to you?" Walt asked.

"Yes, that's fine. I'll head out now." She stood up and grabbed her purse.

"Be cautious." Eddy met her eyes. "We don't know what we're dealing with here."

"I understand, I'll be careful." As she headed out the door, she could feel Eddy's eyes on her. He was always so protective, not just because they were friends, but because she'd confided in him a few times of her adventures as a journalist. She'd pushed the boundaries of safety and sanity on a few occasions. She didn't regret it, but now that she was in her sixties she was a little more cautious about things.

Chapter Six

Samantha took her time as she walked along the hallway of the second floor. Although the hallway was empty, she still listened closely. Voices would drift through the closed doors, and though she doubted that anyone would be discussing a missing body, she listened just in case. As she continued down the hall, her mind shifted back to Eddy's words. He said he checked for a pulse. That was the part that bugged her. Even the best actor couldn't conceal a heartbeat. So, either Eddy was mistaken, which was unlikely to her, or there really was a missing body. She paused outside of the gym and peered inside. There were several types of equipment, televisions, and a vending machine. It was a wide open room, and she didn't see anywhere that a body could be hidden. Still, she opened the door and stepped inside.

In the back of the gym there was a door that

she assumed led to a closet. She tried the knob, but it wouldn't turn. She turned it as hard as she could, and it still didn't budge. With a frown she wished she had Jo's lock-picking skills. She made a note about the closet being a potential hiding place. However, there was nothing else in the room that appeared to be disturbed. With its glass front walls, she guessed that it would be the last place someone would choose to hide a body. There was too much exposure, and too much of a chance that someone could randomly walk in. As she turned to leave she noticed a camera in the corner of the room near the entrance. That was another reason to doubt that the closet was the hiding place. She left the gym and continued down the hall. She checked the other supply closet that she passed. It was filled with cleaning supplies, and an assortment of extra furniture. There was nothing inside it that held her attention. A couple headed towards her from one of the rooms at the end of the hallway. Both looked a little tipsy as they leaned on each other for support.

"Hey, hey!" The man waved his hand at her. "Do you know if they opened up the bar again yet?"

"No sorry, I think it's closed for the night."

"Darn, all because some drunk guy had a breakdown." He chuckled. "Poor sap was probably using more than alcohol. What fun is a blizzard if you can't spend it in a bar?"

"I don't know really." Samantha shrugged. "I've never been in a blizzard before."

"Trust me, you want to be drunk, as drunk as you can be. Just ask my buddy Howard, he'll tell you."

"Oh, is he experienced?"

"Sure, he and I used to hole up in a bar for every blizzard. We practiced our lines, all of the ladies loved it."

"Marty." The woman beside him rolled her eyes. "I don't want to hear about that."

"Sorry hon, but it's true. Me and Howard, we had a blast. You haven't seen him have you?" He rubbed his head for a moment as if he might be confused. "I've been calling him, but he isn't answering."

"I'm sorry, no I haven't."

"Oh well. I bet we can get some booze from room service. Let's go back to your room." He tugged the woman back towards the room. Samantha did her best not to judge. As a rule she tried to accept people as they were. But she had a difficult time with drunks. She turned her attention back to the other rooms in the hallway. As she passed by one room, she noticed that the door was propped open a few inches. She also heard a rather angry voice.

"What do you mean you can't find him? We came all the way here. You promised me that you were the best. You better find him, and fast, or we're going to have a real problem here."

"I've been asking everyone. Someone

mentioned that he pulled a prank on one of the guests, but hasn't been seen since."

"It's not your job to ask questions. It's your job to know the answers. I hired you, for quite a bit of money, and I want results."

"Yes, ma'am, I'm sorry, ma'am."

"Find him."

Samantha ducked out of the way as a tall figure emerged from the room. He didn't appear to be in any mood for introductions as he brushed past her towards the stairs. He wore a long leather coat and a hat with the brim pulled down. It could have just been to protect him from the winter weather, but it struck her as odd that he was wearing it inside. She lingered for a moment close to the door. Maybe if the woman inside came out she would be able to find out some more information. However, after a few minutes slipped by, the door pushed shut and Samantha heard a lock engage. She frowned and continued down the hallway. It sounded like a private argument, not something that she would usually stick her nose into, but in this situation, she felt it was required. Maybe if she could figure out who the woman was, she could find out more about the meaning of the conversation.

***

Eddy checked his watch. Samantha had been gone for a few minutes. He wondered for a moment if he should have gone with her. "I'm headed to the first floor. Let me know if you two come across anything."

"We will." Walt tapped his chin. "I just want to check the plans one more time."

"Good idea." Eddy stepped out the door and closed it behind him.

"Here Jo, I don't want you to go in blind. These are the entrances to the areas that you want to search," Walt said.

"So, do you think through the bar is the best way to access all areas?" Jo leaned over Walt's shoulder and looked at the computer screen.

"I think so. It will give you an entrance to the kitchen, an entrance to the dining hall, and an entrance to that storage room." He pointed out the room on the screen.

"Perfect. It shouldn't be too difficult to get in."

Walt reviewed the floor plans again, then looked over at Jo.

"Are you sure you want to do this alone? I could accompany you."

"Thank you for the offer, Walt, but I can handle it."

"I know you can." He sighed. "I guess it's just in my nature to be protective."

"I appreciate that." She held his eyes for a moment, then tilted her head towards the door. "Let's go. Now is the best time, the sooner the better."

"You're right." He led the way through the door and down to the ground floor. As Jo headed towards the separate wing, Walt trailed behind her.

"Are you going to follow me?" She flashed a smile over her shoulder at him.

"Maybe?"

"I'll be fine, I promise. Just do me a favor, and if you see anyone in the area, keep them occupied."

"I can do that." He nodded. "Just be careful."

"Aw Walt, it's sweet of you to worry about me." She met his eyes.

"Statistically, people who pick locks are far more likely to be shot dead than the average person." He cleared his throat.

"Oh, thanks for that." She raised an eyebrow. "I guess I beat the statistics since I've been picking locks for a very long time, and I'm still here."

"True, you are above average."

"Thanks, Walt." She hugged him, then headed down the hallway towards the wing with the kitchen, dining hall, and bar. Walt paced back and forth through the empty hallways of the ground floor. Most of the ground floor was taken up by the lobby, the recreation room, and a small café and juice bar where breakfast and snacks were sold. The café was closed, the lobby was populated by only one person behind the front desk, and the recreation room was empty. As people sheltered in their rooms for the night, he wondered whether they knew that the murder mystery had already begun. Or was one of them holed up behind a closed door, the killer? His skin crawled at the thought. It was one thing to risk a bedbug infestation, it was quite another to be sharing a roof with a murderer.

When he heard a strange squeaking sound, he followed it down another hallway towards a small section of rooms which from the plans he knew accommodated the staff. The hallway was empty. So where did the sound come from? He walked along the corridor, and listened. He heard a squeak deep inside one of the rooms. As he paused in front of the door, the squeak drew closer. He took a step back just before the door swung open, and a cart was pushed out into the hallway. One of the wheels squeaked.

"I can oil that for you." Walt's eyes widened with desperation. "You don't have to put up with that."

"Excuse me? With what?" The young woman before him stared back.

"That horrible squeak. Just a little bit of oil, or maybe some WD-40, will have it rolling smoothly."

"Oh, I don't even notice it, I guess I'm just used to it."

"You shouldn't have to be." He crouched down and looked at the wheel. "Not to mention what it does to those that have to listen to it as it rolls past. I mean, that kind of grating noise can really wear on the psyche of anyone who is forced to listen to it."

"Are you trying to say that the squeaky wheel on my cart is going to make me crazy?" She laughed. "I'll be sure to tell the boss that. If you don't mind, I have more rooms to clean."

"Oh? What are you using?" He stood back up and eyed the bottles in the top of her cart. "Hmm, not a bad selection, although I would stay away from anything with a pine scent. Research shows that scented cleaning products can cause headaches."

"Huh, really? It doesn't bother me."

"You must have an amazing tolerance level." He studied her for a moment. "Are you a mother?"

"Of two." She smiled.

"That explains it. Mothers are generally too traumatized to be sensitive to small disturbances."

"Traumatized?" She laughed again. "I guess that's one way to put it."

"It's the truth. Your nerves, senses, and stress hormones are so overworked that you become immune to things that used to be intolerable."

"Interesting. I guess that's why I can put up

with all of the screaming."

"Oh yes." He cringed. "I give you credit for that. However, you may want to consider therapy."

"Excuse me?"

"Oh, I mean no offense, I'm just concerned for your mental state. Not enough people are. Mothers are seen as infallible, and as a result many women who are mothers suffer with feelings of hopelessness that are rarely recognized or treated. Do you ever have feelings of hopelessness?"

"Who are you?" She shook her head. "I'm a little concerned about your mental state."

"Oh right, you should be. I have detachment issues and border on obsessive compulsive disorder. But hey, we all have our things, right?"

"Right." She smiled. "As I was saying, I need to move on to the next room."

"Sure, sure. But could I ask you a few questions about your bedbug situation first."

"My bedbug situation?" She blinked.

"Well, not yours personally, although if you work here, it's very likely you could bring them home with you, I was referring to the resort's bedbug situation."

"Okay." She sighed. "But I only have a few minutes."

Chapter Seven

Eddy checked the first floor, but found nothing suspicious. The supply closets were filled with towels, little shampoos, conditioners and other toiletries for the guests. The rest of the floor was guest rooms and there weren't any guests in the hallways. He took the stairs down to the ground floor and walked up them to the third floor. Even though it left him winded, he assumed that the elevators would have cameras. If someone wanted to move a body, they would likely use the stairs. However, by the time he reached the landing of the third floor he hadn't found any sign of foul play. The stairs were dusty, as if they were rarely used, which meant if someone had pulled a body up them, there would be quite a noticeable streak along the wood. Instead things seemed undisturbed, but for the footprints he left behind.

When Eddy emerged on the third floor he

found that there were a few people in the hallway. Two women, and two men. One of the men was dressed in a very fine suit with a suit jacket that draped more like a cape than a jacket. Both women were young, and dressed in short skirts with tight shirts that barely did the job of covering them. The other man was so large he nearly hid both women from view as he stepped in front of them. The tension in his broad shoulders and sharp expression on his face made Eddy think he was accustomed to intimidating others.

"Boss, we're stuck here, there's no way out."

"There has to be a way. Get a helicopter."

"Helicopters don't fly in a blizzard, honey." One of the women leaned on the boss' arm. "We'll just have to find a way to get nice and cozy here."

"Sure baby, we can have..." The other woman leaned on his other arm.

"Enough." He brushed them both off. "I don't want to stay in this hovel. If I say I want a helicopter, I'm going to get a helicopter."

"Boss, there's nowhere to land it. The weather forecast is predicting three feet of snow." The thick man shook his head. "We're stuck."

"Great." The boss sighed.

"All right, go and demand that anyone in rooms near mine get moved. I don't want anyone in my business. Understand, Vinnie?"

"No problem, Boss, I'll get right on it."

"Take care of our little problem first, hmm?" He locked eyes with Vinnie. "You need to find him."

"Yes, I understand." Vinnie opened one of the doors in the hallway for his boss and waited until all three were inside. Then he turned to walk down the hallway. He stopped short when he saw Eddy. "What are you looking at?" He scowled.

"Nothing, just on my way to my room." Eddy hurried past him. He knew better than to take the bait of a man that size. There was no way he could physically compete with him.

As Eddy continued down the hallway he

zeroed in on the two supply closets. When he reached the first one, he tried the doorknob but it was locked. He wiggled the knob a few times but the lock didn't budge. Was it possible that the body was hidden inside? Why else would a simple supply closet be locked? He pulled out his pocket knife and opened the blade. Just as he was about to attempt to pick the lock, he heard footsteps approaching down the hall. He stepped away from the door when he saw it was a staff member. With a nod, he ducked into a short hallway and pretended to be purchasing something from a vending machine. As he perused the options he heard a key slide into the lock. Then the door swung open. He held his breath, though he wasn't quite sure what he expected. Maybe a scream, when the body was discovered? Maybe some kind of guilty utterance? All he heard was the shuffle of boxes, followed by the sound of a key in a lock. As he heard the footsteps fade into the distance, he realized there was no body in that closet.

He moved along down the hallway to the next

closet. When he tried the knob, it turned with ease. He found several shelves of towels inside. There was nowhere to hide a body. With a sigh of frustration he closed the door and continued down the hallway. As he neared the end of it he noticed a sign over one of the doors that indicated stairs. With one quick glance over his shoulder, he opened the door to the stairway. A light flickered above the cement stairs. The walls were bare except for a sign that demanded only authorized personnel should proceed. He ignored the sign and made his way up the stairs. At the landing there was another door, with another sign. He pushed in the long handle on the door, and it opened about an inch, then stopped. He pushed harder, and the door swung open a little further, just enough for him to peer through it.

Cold air blasted him in the face accompanied by snow that swirled so forcefully it began to spill onto the landing. The snow was up to his knees, and essentially blocked the doorway. He shoved his whole body weight against the door, and managed to get it open a few more inches. However, there was no way he could fit through it. Neither could he possibly fit a dead body through it. It occurred to him that if the murderer was quick enough he might have gotten the body outside, and if he did, the snow would have covered it in no time. But that seemed like a huge risk. If someone wanted to hide a body, they wouldn't normally choose to toss it in the snow. Snow melted, eventually. He pulled the door shut and shivered. As he rubbed his hands together to warm them, he wondered if the killer planned to move the body out of the resort, but was surprised by the blizzard. In panic the killer might have been desperate for a place to hide it, which meant he wasn't likely to take it up to the third floor, or the roof. The most likely place he would have hidden it was on the ground floor, in the dining area. But the bar was so crowded at the time of the body's disappearance, would the killer risk being caught? He headed back down to the ground floor. In the hall that led to the bar, he ran into

Walt, who was deep in conversation with a housekeeper.

"But what I'm asking is, how can you guarantee that you're bedbug free if you don't run daily checks on all of the rooms?"

"We run monthly checks on a handful of rooms, and there haven't been any reports of bedbugs, sir."

"But that doesn't mean they're not there. It just means you haven't found them. That's not a guarantee that there aren't any."

"Have you found any bedbugs in your room, sir?" She smiled.

"Well, no. Not yet. But I'm still looking."

"Careful, Walt, or you might just find what you're looking for." Eddy paused beside him. "Instead of what we're actually looking for."

"Oh Eddy, right yes. This is Belinda. She was just telling me about how often the rooms are checked. Now, what if a guest has gone missing? Is there any procedure in place for that?"

"Well, we don't track our guests. People can come and go as they please, unless there is a blizzard of course." She laughed, though her laughter faded when she noticed Eddy's grim expression. "However, if someone is reported as missing then the resort will go into lockdown while the person is searched for. In those cases, it's usually a child or an elderly impaired person that triggers a lockdown. We're not in the business of hunting down angry spouses."

"So, you won't look for someone unless they're vulnerable?"

"Honestly, at that point it's the police's decision. If they feel there is reason to search then of course we will comply with their requests. Is someone you know missing? Could they be outside? I hope not."

"But the police can't get here." Eddy frowned. "They're snowed out, just like we're snowed in."

"Wait a minute, is this about that false claim of a body?" She looked between the two men. "I thought that was just a prank."

"It was no prank. I saw the body, and I know that someone has been killed."

"Oh no!" She gasped and covered her mouth. Then a light giggle escaped her hand. "How was that? I'm trying to get a role in the murder mystery. I've been working on my horrified reaction."

"This is not a joke." Eddy hissed his words through clenched teeth.

"Oh, you're serious?" She shook her head. "Listen, this happens from time to time during these murder mysteries. People underestimate how real it's going to look. They don't think there's going to be blood, or a weapon. They assume there will be some kind of overly dramatic death scene. But that's not how it works. Some people have even called the police, thinking that a real murder has been committed. You're not alone in being shocked by all of this. But it is just acting. Some of the actors have a little competition to see who can be the most realistic victim. They take turns you know. Try not to worry, about that, or the bedbugs." She smiled at Walt, then rolled her cart into the next room. Eddy stared after her. He felt the urge to convince her that he was telling the truth, but he knew that it wouldn't make any real difference.

"Sorry Eddy, if it helps any, she didn't believe me about the bedbugs either."

"Yes Walt, that does help, a little." He sighed. "Have you seen or heard from Jo?"

"No, she said she was turning her phone off so that she wouldn't risk drawing attention to herself."

"I think the killer would have hidden the body somewhere nearby. I don't think he would have risked taking it upstairs."

"Walt! Eddy!" Samantha ran down the hall towards them.

"So much for not drawing attention." Eddy grimaced. "Sam, what is it? Are you okay?"

"Yes!" She tried to catch her breath. "But I just overheard something that might have to do with our victim."

"What is it?"

"Someone, a very angry someone, is looking for a man. She's hired someone to find him, but the man is missing."

"No names?"

"No, I'm sorry, but I know what room she is in."

"Then we can't know for sure if it's our victim, Howard." Walt shrugged.

"No we can't, but if the man she's looking for is missing, and our body is missing, I think we can for the moment assume that they might be one and the same."

"And if she's angry enough to hire someone to find him, she might just be angry enough to kill him." Eddy patted her on the back. "Great job, Sam. Let's hope it can lead us somewhere."

"If we can find out what her name is, that is." Samantha frowned. "I'm not sure that will be so easy, since the security around here is pretty tight."

"We can just do things the old-fashioned way." Eddy grinned. "When I would work a stakeout and we wanted to make sure that the suspect was actually in the room, we would place a fake call from the front desk, and ask for confirmation of their name so that we could send up a complimentary treat. People are always willing to give up information for a treat."

"Oh, what a great idea! I can call the main line and ask to be connected to her room. Then I can pretend to be the front desk."

"Good, see what you can find out, and take Walt with you, make sure you're both out of sight when you make the call. I'm going to see if I can catch up with Jo."

"Okay, I'll make it from my room. What about the rest of the search? I didn't finish the second floor," Samantha said.

"Don't worry about that, we can do it later. If the body is anywhere in this building, I'm getting more and more certain that it's going to be in the separate wing on the ground floor, in the area by the dining hall. I'm going to take a good look around. Anything suspicious, I'm going to check it out." Eddy looked back at his friends. "Good luck, guys."

"Let's go, Samantha." Walt led her back down the hallway towards the stairs. Eddy headed towards the dining hall.

Chapter Eight

Breaking into the bar had been easy. It was a simple lock to pick, and Jo had been careful to point the surveillance camera on the door away before she began to pick it. When she entered the bar, it was empty and the lights were dim. Casually she looked around the areas she hadn't noticed earlier, such as the supply closets and the bathrooms. However, there was nothing to be found. She went through a door behind the bar that led to a large storage space for both the bar and the kitchen, which connected to the space through another door. She had begun her search of the large space when she heard the sound of something hard being kicked across the floor. It had made her stomach sink. There was no question that someone kicked it. It slid, it didn't drop. When the object stopped in front of her she recognized it as a rolling pin. Several more objects crashed or slammed in quick succession, followed by a booming voice.

"I don't want to hear any of your excuses! I don't want to be told what you can't do!"

Jo could hear the tremble in the man's voice and realized just how angry he was. Violently, angry. She hadn't wanted to risk opening the door to the bar as it might let in light, or make a sound. Instead she had climbed into the open cabinet of a rolling cart, and pulled the door closed behind her. Jo crouched down in the cabinet and held her breath. Squashed into a squatting position, she pressed her hands against the metal sides of the cabinet to keep her hands from shaking. As the voice continued to carry through the open space, it seemed even louder in the small cabinet. "I've warned the three of you, if you don't find him and handle this, I'm going to handle you. You got us into this mess, and you're going to get us out."

"We couldn't have expected the blizzard. You can't blame us for that." A thin whiny voice responded. Another loud crash followed his words, followed by a cry of pain.

"Anyone else want to argue with me? We have

to get out of this. No excuses, only solutions." She heard heavy footsteps draw close to the cabinet. With every step her heart shuddered. Would he notice her breathing? Would he open the cabinet for some reason? Finally, the footsteps continued past. She heard the door to the bar open and close. She breathed a sigh of relief. Then, to her surprise, the cart lurched. It rolled forward. The door to the bar opened again, and the cart rolled forward.

"He didn't have to break his nose."

"Carlisle does whatever he wants to do. You know that. Jamie knew better than to question him."

"But he was right. We couldn't have expected the snow, could we? It's not like we control the weather."

"That's not the point. The point is that no matter what happens, we need to be able to fix it. So you either do that, you fix it, or you stop complaining. If you're going to keep on complaining, then you'll end up dead."

"Great. If the pay wasn't so good, I'd quit."

"There's no quitting."

"I know." He grunted. "All right, what did they order?"

"A bottle of rum, two glasses, and a bottle of soda."

"Great. I'll get the rum and the glasses, you get the soda."

Jo could hardly draw a breath as she realized they might open the door to the cabinet to put the items inside. She grabbed the inside edge of the door and held on to it as tight as she could. Right after she did, one of the men tried to open it. The cabinet door almost jerked out from under her fingertips, but she clung on as tight as she could. These two men worked for a man who considered death to be the only way out of his employment, she didn't want to be caught eavesdropping."

"Barney, what's the hold up?"

"This stupid thing won't open." Barney tugged at the door again.

"Kick it."

"I'm not going to kick it, what's that going to do, Kent? It'll just get it even more stuck."

"Whatever, just put the stuff on top. Solutions, right?"

"Solutions." Barney stopped tugging on the door. Jo relaxed a little, but not much. She couldn't, as the muscles in her legs trembled from being stuck in the same position for so long. Even though she wanted to believe that she was as limber as she once was, her muscles begged to differ. The cart began to roll again. She wondered if she shoved the door open and rolled out would that create enough of a diversion for her to escape unharmed. She didn't really want to risk it and find out. The cart stopped. She heard the sound of the elevator doors. She knew if they got on the elevator, she would really have no way out.

"What the heck is in this thing? It's heavy." One of the men grunted as he tried to roll the cart onto the elevator.

"I don't know. Like I said, the door is stuck. I'm going to check in with Jamie."

"All right, I'll take care of this."

Jo saw the door start to move. She grabbed it just in time. Then the entire door shook. The strike of the man's foot against the door made her ears ring.

"Hey, what's all of the commotion about?"

Jo's eyes widened at the familiar voice. Eddy, it was Eddy.

"Just trying to get this door open, it's stuck. Sorry to disturb you."

"Here, let me give you a hand." Eddy walked over to him. The cabinet on the cart looked big enough to hide a body, if it was contorted into a pretzel. A cart would be the easiest way to transport a body throughout the resort as well.

"No, that's all right, I can handle it."

"Well, kicking it isn't going to work. I saw someone from the maintenance staff down the hall. Why don't you go see if he has something to force it open? I'll stay with the cart so no one steals your stuff."

"I don't know." He frowned.

"Okay, you can just keep kicking it." Eddy shrugged.

"All right, all right, I'll go grab the staff member."

As soon as he walked off, Eddy reached for the door. But before he could grab it, the door popped open. Eddy gasped and stumbled backwards as Jo sprang forward and nearly bumped into him.

"Oops, sorry Eddy." Jo caught herself on the wall, then caught him by the elbow to steady him. "You have no idea how glad I am to see you."

"I think I have some idea." He quirked a brow. "What were you doing in there?"

"Not now, we need to get out of here before those guys come back. They're bad news." She quickly turned the camera by the bar door back to the position she had found it in.

"They were just delivering room service."

"That might be what they're pretending to do, but trust me, that's not what is happening here. We need to go."

"All right, let's go back to your room, Walt and Samantha are already there."

"Okay." Jo grimaced as her sore legs struggled to support her. She wasn't sure exactly how long she'd been in the cabinet, but she knew that it was long enough to cause quite a bit of pain. They walked into the room just as Samantha hung up the phone.

"Jennifer Candin, that's the woman in room 217." She turned to face Eddy and Jo.

"Interesting, but what's even more interesting, is where I found Jo. She was wedged into the cabinet of a metal cart."

"What?" Samantha rushed over to her. "Are you okay?"

"I opened the door expecting to find a dead body, and out popped Jo."

"Jo, it's not good for you to put so much strain on your body." Walt studied her.

"I think it would have been worse for those four men to get their hands on me. That would have put a lot more strain on my body."

"Oh Jo! What happened?" Samantha grabbed her hand.

"I broke into the bar, as planned. Then went into the shared storage space, and there was a guy in there throwing a full on temper tantrum. He was kicking things, throwing things, he broke the nose of one of his men."

"What guy?" Eddy narrowed his eyes.

"I'm sorry, I don't know, I think they called him Carlisle. But whoever he was, he was bad. The men working under him were terrified of him, basically under the threat of death if they disobeyed. He was very upset with them." She recounted the conversation as well as she could remember it.

"That sounds similar to what I overheard.

Except, in my case, it wasn't as violent," Eddy said.

"It seems to me that several people are missing one particular man. Do you think it's possible that they're all looking for the same person, the victim that we're looking for?" Walt looked between his friends.

"I'm not sure. No one actually said his name. Actually, one person did. A man who was very drunk. He mentioned to me that he was looking for Howard, and said that they always get drunk together during blizzards," Samantha said.

"Our Howard?" Eddy raised an eyebrow.

"I think it must be. He said that his friend was an actor in the murder mystery as well."

"So he's a drunk, like the head of security claimed." Jo frowned. "Maybe he really is just missing."

"If he's a drunk and just missing, he certainly has a lot of enemies looking for him," Walt said.

"We don't know that yet. No one said for sure

who they were looking for." Samantha began to pace. "I think we need to spend some time finding out as much as we can about Howard. Clearly, we're not going to find his body."

"Are you back to thinking there never was a body?" Eddy sighed.

"No, I'm not thinking that at all. But what I am thinking is that at this point it's going to be easier to focus on who might have killed Howard, instead of where his body is. Finding his body isn't really going to change much is it?"

"At least the security team will start taking me more seriously." Eddy crossed his arms.

"Maybe, but they still won't be able to bring the police in, we're snowed in. Not much will change if we find the body, other than that the murderer will know that he or she is about to get caught," Samantha said.

"That's true. As long as there is no evidence of a crime the murderer is going to feel confident, as if the crime will never be solved. That will change the moment the body is found," Jo said.

"And let's keep in mind that by tomorrow afternoon, if Howard doesn't turn up, people are going to start putting two and two together on their own. I mean, where else could he be? No one can leave." Walt opened his computer. "Let's find out what we can about Howard."

"A last name would be a good start," Eddy said.

"I might know how to get that," Samantha said. "Can you search the murder mystery on the computer, Walt. It might have the names of the actors."

"Sure." Walt typed away on the computer. "Bingo! Howard Brance."

"Good work, Walt!" Eddy glanced at his watch. "I'll see if I can find someone to talk to about Howard, but it's getting late."

"Can I quickly use your computer first to do some research on Jennifer Candin?" Samantha looked at Walt.

"Of course."

"And I am going to take a bath." Jo rubbed her arms. "I need to relax my muscles after that tight fit. Does anyone mind?"

"No, of course not. Be sure to wash the tub out first though, who knows who bathed in there last." Walt shuddered.

"Thanks for that, Walt." Jo rolled her eyes. "If you find anything out just let us know, Eddy, I can be out of the bath in a snap."

"Don't worry about it, Jo. We probably won't have much to go on until tomorrow. I'll find out what I can about Howard though," Eddy said.

When Eddy left the room he could feel a pressure building deep inside him. For the first time he questioned himself. Was it possible that he didn't see what he thought he saw? All of his friends were supporting him, but what if he was wrong? Maybe Howard really was alive, and the entire search had been a waste of what could have been relaxation time.

Chapter Nine

On his way to the lobby, Eddy paused in the dining hall. It was still empty. He stared at the place on the floor where he'd first seen the body. The memory of it flashed through his mind. In that second, he realized that he'd seen Howard before. In the bar. He refused the offer of an alcoholic drink from Ben, the bartender. He just wanted water. But the person Samantha talked to, claimed he was a heavy drinker. That was a little odd. But the more he thought about it, the more certain he was that the body on the floor belonged to the same man he'd seen in the bar. He shivered as he realized he was one of the last people to see Howard alive.

As Eddy turned to leave the dining hall he noticed a shadow cast by someone in the adjoining hallway. For an instant he froze. He thought he was alone, and hadn't even sensed that there was someone else there. That was unusual for him. Maybe his instincts really were off. As he rounded the corner he nearly walked into the man who approached. He recognized him right away. It was the bartender.

"Hey, Eddy right?"

"Yes. Ben?"

"You've got it. What are you doing out wandering this late?"

"I'm having a hard time sleeping."

"Oh, that's right, you're the one that thought you saw a body, right?" He locked eyes with Eddy. "What exactly did you see?"

"I saw a body, Howard's body, to be specific."

"Howard, the actor?"

"Yes, the man who was in your bar not long before I saw him dead on the floor in the dining hall."

"But it was a mistake." Ben chuckled. "Obviously, dead men don't get up and walk away."

"They're not supposed to be able to, no. However, that does appear to be what happened here."

"Maybe he's a zombie?" Ben laughed again.

"I doubt that. But I do think that someone managed to move the body before I had the chance to get help. Maybe you could tell me a little bit about Howard. Did you know him well?"

"Pretty well. I mean, I know all of the actors pretty well. They like to hang out in the bar."

"I noticed that Howard declined your offer for a drink. Was he sober?"

"I doubt it. He'd been talking about it, but no one really took him seriously. In fact, my best bet as to where he is right this second, would be that he's passed out somewhere, sleeping off a very large amount of alcohol."

"So, you think he wasn't being serious in the bar? He was just putting on a show?"

"Maybe. It's hard to say for sure. This is his first show back after some time off so maybe he did change, but I doubt it. But anyway, he isn't the most reliable. He is always making some kind of declaration, but then he doesn't follow through with it."

"I bet that upset quite a few people. Did you notice him having problems with anyone in particular?"

"You'd be better off asking who he doesn't have problems with. Everyone is after Howard."

"What do you mean?"

"He's in debt up to his eyeballs, from what I understand, and to dangerous people."

"Like?"

"Like loan sharks, and casinos, and anyone who has ever loaned him money."

"Poor guy, sounds like he's had a rough time."

"He brings it on himself. He gets drunk, and makes bad choices. Then everyone else has to pay for it. I can't tell you how many times he didn't show up in time for a show or a rehearsal."

"That must upset his co-workers."

"Yes, it does. But most of them are used to it. If he doesn't show up they just scramble to find someone to cover him."

"Why doesn't he get fired?"

"Because, he's a really good actor. Even though they get annoyed with him, no one wants him gone."

"Well, at least he has one talent then."

"Yes, he does." Ben frowned. "Sorry if it sounds like I'm putting him down. It's just that I want you to understand, if you made a mistake, it's not your fault. He's a great actor, and an even more talented drunk."

"I appreciate that, but I didn't make a mistake. Do you think there's some way I could speak with the other actors in his group?"

"Sure. They have breakfast together in the café at six on show days. If you are willing to get up early you can catch them for autographs."

"Great. I think I'll do that." Eddy nodded his head. "What about a girlfriend? He must have someone around here that he likes to spend time with."

"No one in particular that I know of. He used to spend time with a few different women, but I rarely saw him with a woman more than a few times. Lately, I haven't seen him with anyone."

"All right, thanks for the information."

"Sure. Like I said, don't be down on yourself. Everyone makes mistakes, especially around here. Come see me after lunch tomorrow, I'll hook you up with a great dark beer that I only keep for special customers."

"That sounds delicious. Thanks again." Eddy headed back to the second floor. As determined as he was to solve the case he realized he'd hit a dead end for the night. No one was going to give him any more information even if he managed to wake them up. Instead he headed back to the room.

Chapter Ten

Samantha only had to dig a little bit in order to get a lead on Jennifer. "Well, it's not too hard to figure out who Jennifer Candin is." She sat back in the chair, and looked up at Walt. "She is Howard's ex-wife."

"How did you find that out?" Walt pulled up a chair beside her.

"It wasn't hard. She has a public profile online, and she listed more than one last name. I followed that to the record of her marriage, and discovered that she's recently divorced from Howard Brance."

"Wow. That sounds like motive to me."

"There's more. It seems that the divorce was pretty messy. I should say, it was a massacre."

"Oh? How so?"

"From what I gathered from her rants, he was a drunk with a gambling problem. He gambled most of their savings. She won everything in the divorce. House, car, cat."

"Oh, not the cat." Walt chuckled.

"I was also able to get some financial information on him from one of my old contacts. So you can use your magic skills to use that information to get more information."

"Well done!" It always surprised Walt how Samantha managed to get information. Her past as an investigative journalist still meant she had some very handy contacts.

"Thanks." Samantha smiled at his enthusiasm.

"Okay, let me work my magic and I'll see what I can find out about their financial situations. It seems pretty clear that Howard was left with nothing, but if that's the case, what motive would Jennifer have to kill him?"

"Maybe just the bitterness over a bad marriage?" She frowned. "But it does seem odd that she would go to all of this trouble to hunt him down, just to kill him. I don't see how she benefits from it, unless she just wanted to settle a score of some kind."

"I guess that's also a possibility. Maybe he hurt her so much that she wanted revenge. Maybe there were things that went on in their marriage that she can't forgive and move on from. It's not logical, but relationships aren't always logical."

"That's for sure." Samantha switched into Walt's seat so that he could sit in front of the computer. She barely noticed as he wiped off the keyboard before he began to type. Walt's habits rarely drew her attention anymore. Now that Walt had Howard's full name and some financial records, it wasn't hard for him to begin to pull together his financial profile. One of the first things that he noticed was that Howard had several closed accounts on his credit report. Some were in good standing, but most were due to lack of funds, and some had fees piling up. His credit was low as a result of missed payments, and also several open and maxed credit cards.

"This isn't looking good for Howard." Walt frowned. "This man was losing money left and right."

"I imagine he must be paid pretty well for his role here."

"You would think, but as it looks right now, I'm not seeing anything but loss. I'm not sure where he's putting his paychecks, but none of it is being used to pay off his debts. I can't track his recent spending, because none of it seems to have been done through a bank account or credit card. The only thing I did find on him recently is that he purchased a plane ticket. However, I don't think that the ticket was for him. It was for someone else."

"Jennifer?"

"I don't know. All I know is that the flight originated in Colorado, and flew here. There's no record of a flight out, so I can only assume that someone was flying in."

"Maybe."

Walt continued to skim through the information that he found. When he clucked his tongue, Samantha looked over at him.

"What is it?"

"It appears that our friend had a problem with a casino. I see several legal actions taken against him by one casino in particular, Sheron's."

"Sheron's? Isn't that in Nevada?"

"Yes, it is."

"Any evidence that Howard was in Nevada?"

"Let me take a look." As Walt continued to search, the door to the room swung open. Eddy walked in and sat down at the table with them, but remained silent as Walt held up a finger. After some time, Walt lowered it. "It appears that Howard was engaging in online gambling, which explains what happened to his paychecks. Sheron's offers a direct payment service and paychecks can be deposited electronically into the system."

"He was depositing his entire paycheck into a

gambling account?" Samantha gasped. "He must have been drunk to do something like that."

"That's what he was doing, until he lost big, I don't see any record of any further deposits. However, he has an outstanding balance of three hundred thousand dollars."

"Three hundred thousand?" Eddy looked between the two of them. "That's a huge amount of dough."

"Yes it is, and the owner of Sheron's has a reputation for ensuring that all debts are paid. The posts I'm reading are vague, but all imply violence."

"I wonder if that might have been who Eddy overheard in the hallway," Samantha said.

"It could be. Would a casino owner come all this way to collect?" Eddy shook his head. "Seems like a stretch."

"Maybe for most, but Tad Billings, the owner of Sheron's, is known for taking things personally," Walt said.

"One of the men I overheard on the third floor had a very powerful demeanor. So, maybe Sam is right and it was him," Eddy said.

"Now that we have some names we might be able to check the guest registry." Samantha jotted down the name of the owner of Sheron's. "If he owes money to so many people, the suspect list could be endless."

"True, but the thing to keep in mind is that whoever killed Howard, did so in this resort, and is very likely still trapped here in this resort," Eddy said.

"Don't forget about the wife." Jo stepped out of the bathroom. She rubbed a towel through her hair. "Sorry, I was listening in. We know the ex-wife is here, we don't know who else is here. It's possible the guys in the storage room were from a casino, and just as possible that they work for a loan shark. The key is, everyone wanted money from Howard."

"Even the wife?" Eddy stood up from the

table. "Did he swindle her out of a settlement?"

"No actually. The wife made out very well in the divorce." Walt tapped his fingertips together. "We considered that perhaps the motive had more to do with emotion than with money."

"Maybe." Eddy shook his head. "Without more information, there's nowhere we can go with any of this."

"I think our best solution at the moment might be to call it a night." Samantha stifled a yawn. "Our minds will be sharper in the morning, and maybe by that time, the security team will have come to their senses."

"Let's hope so." Eddy nodded to Walt. "Let's allow the ladies their privacy. We'll meet in the café in the morning? Six? I was told the actors will be there. It will be a good time to question them."

"Good plan." Jo walked with them to the door. "And be careful, Eddy. As of right now, you're the only one that saw that body. The killer might be watching you."

"I'll be careful."

"Good night, Walt."

"Good night, Jo, Samantha. Don't forget to check your mattresses!"

Jo pushed the door closed and turned back to Samantha in time for them to exchange grins at Walt's dedication.

"He's passionate, that's for sure." Samantha shook her head.

"Yes, he is." Jo wiped a hand across her forehead. "I'm exhausted."

"Me too. I hope the morning brings some clarity to all of this."

"Sam."

"Yes?"

"You do think there was a body, right?"

"Yes, I do." Samantha sat down on the edge of her bed. "If Eddy says there was, I believe him."

"Good. I do, too. I just hope he believes that we believe him."

"Me too."

Chapter Eleven

When Eddy woke up the next morning, the events of the day before struck him before he even opened his eyes. His thoughts were plagued with the memory of Howard's body and who his killer might be. As he climbed out of bed he found Walt by the window with a cup of tea.

"Walt, did you sleep at all?"

"Yes, but I got up early, it's the easiest way not to miss anything. We only have about twenty minutes before we need to be down at the café."

"All right, I'm going to grab a quick shower to help wake me up. Or do you need to go first?"

"Already did, and scrubbed the shower down, so you're good to go."

"Thanks Walt."

"I've also been looking into Howard's financial records a little deeper. I discovered that he's worked for this acting company fairly steadily for the past two years."

"Fairly steadily?"

"I can only assume that the breaks in employment are due to his drinking problem."

"That would explain things. But somehow he always ends up back here. I wonder if there might be a reason for that?"

"He must have a good relationship with his boss, to still have his job."

"All right, I'll be out shortly." Eddy disappeared into the bathroom. Walt continued to dig through what he could find about Howard. With a bit of effort he was able to access a copy of the divorce agreement between Howard and Jennifer. Outlined in the agreement was what Howard needed to pay Jennifer. He skimmed over the usual alimony, the house, and froze when he saw another entry that detailed a ninety thousand dollar savings account that was to be turned over to Jennifer. However, he couldn't find any record of the money being transferred to her.

In fact he found records of her filing law suits in an attempt to get the money. By the time Eddy emerged from the shower, Walt had run out of time to search. They met up with Jo and Samantha in the hallway.

"I found something odd in Howard's divorce agreement with his ex-wife. It seems to me that ninety thousand dollars might be missing."

"That sounds like a pretty good motive for murder." Samantha pushed the button on the elevator. The doors slid open and the four stepped inside.

"Yes, it does. And, she's here. So obviously she was up to something."

"What about those men in the storage room, though?" Jo narrowed her eyes. "They were vicious."

"True, but we don't know for sure who they were after." Walt led the way out of the elevator.

"And the man I ran into in the hallway was pretty intense, too." Eddy trailed after his three friends as they headed towards the café. He couldn't help but stare into the dining hall as they passed it. Everything was undisturbed. There was still no sign of a murder. No police tape, no memorial, nothing. His stomach twisted at the thought. They were almost to the café, when Bart walked up to them.

"Morning, you're all up early."

"We have a murder mystery to solve, don't we?" Eddy smiled.

"Like I said, we didn't find a body yet to lead us to believe there was a crime of any kind committed. However, we also have yet to find Howard. I thought perhaps you could take a look at this picture for me, and see if you think it was who you saw last night."

Eddy gritted his teeth. Several words flew through his mind that he would have liked to say out loud, but he decided against it.

"Sure." He gazed at the picture on Bart's cell phone. "Yes, that's the man I saw last night."

"Okay." Bart shut his phone off and tucked it back into his pocket. "At this point, because of his reckless behavior, the resort has decided it will press charges against him. The manager would like to speak with you directly and apologize for the disturbance."

"Instead of pressing charges against a dead man, why not consider that Eddy could be right?" Samantha studied the man before her.

"It is hard to consider that when no body has been found."

"Are you aware that Howard's ex-wife is staying in this resort? Or that he owed large amounts of money to ruthless debtors?"

"Uh, well. No, I wasn't aware of that." Bart frowned.

"While you assumed that Howard was just missing, we've been trying to figure out why he might have been killed. Trust me, it is more likely that someone murdered him, than it is that Eddy made a mistake."

"But without evidence..."

"Without evidence we have no proof." Walt nodded. "But we still need to investigate based on what we do know. Sometimes you have to take the risk of being wrong, in order to find the truth. Something to consider."

"I'll review whatever security footage I can find throughout the resort." Bart shook his head. "I'm not saying there was a crime, but if there was, it would be best to find out as fast as possible."

"Yes, it would be." Eddy held his gaze. "Because if, as you say there might have been a crime, which as I say there was, then you have bigger problems than a body in your resort. You have a murderer, snowed in with the rest of your guests."

Bart's eyes widened. He turned and walked away.

"I think he's starting to catch on." Jo crossed her arms. "Maybe we'll be getting some help with this soon."

"There might be something on the surveillance footage. There are plenty of cameras around here." Samantha led the rest of the way to the café. The cast members of the murder mystery were gathered around two small tables pushed together. Samantha counted seven members, and guessed that the only one missing was Howard.

"Good morning." She smiled at them. "I'm here with the group from Sage Gardens, who you will be performing for today."

"How nice." A woman with long, blonde hair, and sharp features, held out her hand to Samantha. "I am the host of the murder mystery today, Denise. It's a pleasure to meet you."

"Samantha." She shook her hand and smiled. "I'm sure that you will all put on a wonderful show."

"It's more than a show to us, we take it quite seriously." An older man, with a gruff tone looked from Samantha to the others gathered behind her. "We're not ready for autographs yet."

"Victor, don't be so rude." Denise rolled her eyes. "They're just saying hello."

"Will you be able to continue with the performance? I understand one of your actors is missing." Eddy kept his gaze on Victor. If he took acting so seriously, perhaps he'd had enough of Howard's flaky ways?

"We have all played the different roles more than once. Howard is one of our best victims, but he can be replaced." Victor's lip curled into a mild smirk. "It's not the first time he's been a no-show."

"It's ridiculous." A younger man on the opposite side of the table from Victor shook his head. "I just can't believe he would do this." Samantha noticed Marty, the man that was looking for Howard the previous night, sitting next to the younger man.

"Try not to worry about it, Jeremiah, it's just how Howard is. Once you get to know him, you'll understand." A petite, black-haired woman reached out and patted Jeremiah's hand. Jeremiah pulled his hand away and narrowed his eyes.

"I'm not worried about it, Callie, I just think it's irresponsible and unprofessional."

"Well, maybe if you hadn't gotten into a fight with him last night, he'd be here this morning and we wouldn't be having this conversation." Denise crossed her legs under the table and fixed Jeremiah with a steady glare.

"That's not why he's not here." Jeremiah flipped his hair out of his eyes and stared off in the other direction.

"Sounds like there were some issues?" Eddy frowned. "Co-workers sometimes struggle to get along."

"The only way to get along with Howard is to accept him for who he is. Actors are a different breed. They are whimsical, irrational, and impulsive. We all are. Howard's no different," Callie said.

"Oh, that's the excuse?" Jeremiah stood up from the table. "I don't want to listen to this anymore. I'll be back in time for rehearsal." He stalked off, out of the café. Samantha glanced at Jo, who nodded. Then Samantha followed after Jeremiah. Jo sat down in Jeremiah's empty seat.

"I have to admit I am fascinated by actors. I once thought about going into acting myself."

"Oh really?" Callie smiled. "You have the bone structure for it."

"Acting isn't all about being pretty enough, Callie." Another woman beside her huffed. "It's about talent, imagination, and dedication."

"That's true, Marsha." Victor nodded. "You have to forgive Jeremiah, he's young, and hasn't been involved in the acting life long."

"Is there a reason why he and Howard argued?" Jo glanced between them. Eddy and Walt stood back as Jo blended right in with the group.

"Howard has been on this kick lately,

claiming that he's not drinking anymore. But it's just one of his usual ploys." Denise waved her hand dismissively.

"I really thought he was going to pull it off this time." Marsha sighed.

"Usual ploys? Did he have a habit of swearing off things?" Jo asked.

"He had a habit of doing everything." Callie giggled. "The man manages to get addicted to anything and everything. Cards, ponies, alcohol, you name it."

"Callie, watch it." Victor rapped his hand on the table. "Gossip is the fastest way to create a problem."

"It's not gossip if it's true, Victor." Denise laughed.

"Anyway, Jeremiah is a bit of a straight arrow. He thinks acting should be treated like religion, pure and obedient. He doesn't yet know what real acting requires from a person. So, when he found out that Howard fell off the wagon, he was upset.

Thought he could strong arm him into behaving himself. But the thing with Howard is that he doesn't take direction well. If he did, he would have been in the movies, not in some little murder mystery."

"Hey, it's a very highly acclaimed little murder mystery." Denise sniffed.

"Everyone at this table knows that Howard is the real star here. If he ever gets his life together, he'll be famous," Callie said.

"Had anyone else been upset with him lately? Did he know his ex-wife was here?" Jo watched for the reactions of the people at the table.

"Oops." Callie giggled again. "I guess everybody knows now."

"Callie? What did you do?" Marsha frowned.

"All I did was come to the aid of a woman scorned. We all know that Howard has been doing his best to hide from her."

"You just love to cause drama, don't you, Callie?" Denise sighed. "Acting isn't enough for you, you need the real life soap opera, too?"

"It does make things interesting, doesn't it?" Callie shrugged.

"Do you know if Howard met with Jennifer since she's been here?" Jo held Callie's gaze.

"I don't know anything about anything." She widened her eyes. "I'm just the messenger, I delivered the message, whatever happened after that is not my business."

"No wonder Howard took off. This is your fault, Callie!" Victor stood up from the table. "No matter how many of us you pick off, you're never going to be the star of this show."

"Everyone, just settle down." Jo placed a hand on Victor's shoulder. "I'm sure we can figure all of this out if we work together."

"Ha!" Victor snorted. "I have no interest in working with this woman. She is a con artist and a traitor. Why would you tell Jennifer that he was here?"

"Because he stole her money. That was her

money. She earned it, and she deserved to have it. He gambled it away, and the poor woman was about to lose her house. Was she supposed to just endure that?"

"Did Howard know she was coming?" Jo asked.

"No. He didn't. But when Jennifer got here, I told him. I didn't want him to be totally blindsided," Callie said.

"So that's why he took off. He wanted to get away from his ex. Mystery solved." Victor waved his hand through the air. "Anything else you want from us?"

"No, that should do." Eddy slid his hands into his pockets. "Just keep in mind that there may be more to Howard's disappearance than you assume."

"Don't worry, my friend, if we hear a word from our dear Howard, you will be the first to know." Denise patted his hand.

"Thank you." Eddy nodded as he turned away.

Walt followed after him, but Jo lingered.

"I'm looking forward to your show."

"Good." Denise smiled. "I'm sure that you will enjoy it. We really do work hard to make sure that it's as entertaining as possible. I know right now you probably see us as chaotic and competitive, but the truth is, we're really all a family. We may have our problems, just like any family, but when it comes down to it, we would do anything for each other."

"Anything?" Jo looked between the faces around the table.

"Just as you would look out for your friends, we look out for ours. If any of us truly believed that Howard was in any trouble, we'd all be hunting down the person who hurt him."

"That's good to know. Good luck today, with the show."

"Thank you. Good luck with solving the mystery."

Jo followed after Eddy and Walt. They stood

close to the tall front windows of the lobby.

"It's amazing isn't it?" Eddy gazed out the window. "Millions of snowflakes, and each one is unique."

"That actually isn't exactly true. While no two snowflakes are identical, many are very similar. In fact thirty-five types of snowflakes have been identified so far." Walt sighed. "But, they are all still quite exquisite."

"Interesting, but that doesn't solve our murder." Jo looked back over her shoulder at the actors. "It's hard to decide what to believe and not believe about that group. They're trained to pretend and create illusion."

"They seemed pretty raw to me." Eddy shrugged. "Lots of infighting. I think if one of them had something to do with it, it won't be long before something leaks out."

"Too bad we don't have much time to wait." Jo looked back out at the snow that was still falling. "We may be snowed in now, but the blizzard is forecast to let up tonight or tomorrow. Then the roads will be cleared. We're on a deadline if we want to find Howard's killer."

Chapter Twelve

"Jeremiah, wait." Samantha caught up with him as he neared the elevator.

"What is it?" He turned to look at her. She was startled to see tears in his eyes. "I don't have time for autographs right now."

"No, of course not. You're quite upset. Is there anything I can do?"

"No, there's nothing. I just made some bad decisions and now I'm paying the price."

"What kind of bad decisions?"

"What do you care?" He sighed and wiped at his eyes. "I'm sorry, I don't mean to be rude. I know that you're just being considerate. But there's nothing that you can do for me. I never should have come here in the first place." He stepped into the elevator.

"If you want to talk about it, Jeremiah, I could listen. I'm very good at that."

"Thanks, but no thanks." The elevator doors slid shut. Samantha stared at the doors for a moment. She was tempted to follow after him. It seemed odd to her that he would become so emotional over an argument with another actor. Maybe he knew what the other actors didn't, that Howard really was dead. If that was the case, then he was likely the murderer. She made a note to look into Jeremiah. She wanted to know where he came from, and what his connection to Howard was. As she turned back towards the café, her friends walked towards her.

"Anything from Jeremiah?" Eddy paused in front of her.

"Only that he's very upset over something. I doubt that it's just about that one argument. I want to find out more about him."

"And how about Callie?" Jo scrunched up her nose. "She directed Jennifer right to Howard. Maybe Howard found out and confronted her about it. She could have killed him during the fight."

"Maybe, but any kind of yelling and screaming would have been heard, don't you think?" Eddy frowned.

"Not necessarily." Walt held up a finger. "If the murder took place during the time we think it did, the bar was quite crowded and loud, and there was loud music on. There is a very good chance that any shouting or cries for help would not have been heard by anyone inside the bar."

"Good thought." Eddy shoved his hands in his pockets. "Well, if there's one thing I've learned through years of investigating, it's that the bartender always knows more than he reveals. I'm going to speak with Ben again. Maybe he knows something about the argument between Howard and Jeremiah. Someone had to have seen or heard something."

"Oh my, I think we did!" Samantha's mouth dropped open for a second. "Remember? Last night at dinner?"

"Oh, that's right, it looked like two of the

actors were having a heated discussion, maybe even an argument. That could have been Howard. I didn't really pay attention," Jo said.

"Yes, it could have been. We should talk with the wait staff of the dining hall as well. They may have seen or heard more than we did." Samantha glanced between them. "I think it's going to be best if we split this up. I'll research Jeremiah, and see if I can find a connection with Howard." Samantha pulled out her phone to make a few more notes.

"I'll talk to Ben since we already know each other fairly well," Eddy said. "Jo, do you think you could find out from Bart the names of everyone on the wait staff?"

"I doubt it, but I can try. Plus, anyone that was working last night, has to still be here. I can try to find out exactly where they're staying and talk to whoever is available."

"Good. Walt, maybe you could use what you know about Jennifer and Howard's divorce to get some more information from her."

"Sure, I'll give it a try."

"Let's not forget about the loan shark and casino angle. Jo, can you find out from Bart if any high profile criminal types are staying here? He should have been aware of that if they are."

"Sure, if he'll talk to me."

"I'm sure he will. Didn't you see the way he was looking at you?"

"Whatever, Eddy, I could be his mother."

"Hardly." Samantha clucked her tongue. "He's at least in his forties."

"And?" Jo laughed. "All right, I'll do my best."

"Let's meet back in the dining hall for lunch. Remember, everyone be careful. Howard's murderer is not exactly going to like people asking questions about him." Eddy looked between each of them. "Don't take this lightly. We're going to solve this, but there are a lot of dangerous people under this roof."

As Eddy, Samantha, and Jo headed out to their assignments, Walt tried to ignore his racing heartbeat. Could he really handle talking to Jennifer? What if he slipped up and revealed too much? After a few deep breaths he did his best to focus on the task. Then he checked his reflection in the mirror. He made sure that every hair was in place, his glasses were straight, and that his collar was smooth. Once he was satisfied with the way he looked, he stepped out of his room and walked down the hallway. When he reached room 217 he paused outside and listened. If anyone was inside, they weren't making any noise. After a swift but heavy knock he waited for Jennifer to answer. After he wiped off his knuckles, he took a breath, and counted down from thirty. When Jennifer didn't come to the door, he knocked again, this time a little harder. The door swung open before he had a chance to wipe his knuckles again.

"What is it?" Jennifer stared into his eyes. He recognized her from the photographs he'd found online of her. She was a pretty woman with strong features and shoulder-length blonde hair. Walt could tell from the color tint that it was dyed, but the shade suited her.

"My name is Walt, I was wondering if I could ask you a few questions."

"About what?" She narrowed her eyes. "Is this some kind of religious thing? Does that even happen at places like this?"

"No, not religious. I am here about your ex-husband, Howard."

"Oh? Do you know where he is?"

"That's something I'm trying to find out. I thought you might be able to help me with that."

"You're one of a long list of people that are trying to find Howard. I know he's here somewhere in this resort, but I haven't been able to pin him down. He's slippery."

"Why are you looking for him?"

"Because he owes me money from our divorce settlement, money that wasn't even his to begin with. I'm sure he doesn't have it, with all of his gambling, but I need him to sign a piece of paper attesting to that so that I can initiate a lawsuit. One of these days that buffoon is going to hit it rich in Hollywood and I want my money back when he does."

"I can understand that. A man owes what he owes. Perhaps though, he didn't want to sign that paper."

"I wouldn't know if he wanted to sign it or not, because I haven't found him. Apparently he's missing. But I suppose you already know that, or you wouldn't be here talking to me. Did you talk to Carlisle yet? Or Tad?"

"Uh, no I haven't. You're the first person I've spoken to. Are the others looking for him as well?"

"Sure, and Howard better hope I find him first, because if Carlisle finds him he's dead, and if Tad finds him he's just going to disappear off the face of the earth."

"They sound like dangerous men. How do you

know them?"

"How do I know them?" She rolled her eyes. "By making the worst mistake of my life and marrying Howard. I used to be a normal person, with a future, and a good savings account. But I fell for Howard and I believed his lies. As a result, I got introduced to some of the seediest characters out there. I didn't ask for these people to be in my life, but in the pursuit of Howard they have destroyed my property, my sanity and any chance I had at a good credit rating. So, if you want to find Howard you're going to have to wait your turn."

"I'm not here to compete, I'm here to offer my help. I have some very good research skills and with a little information from you I might just be able to figure out where he took off to."

"I don't need your help. I hired my own help. I have a private detective on the case, and he has assured me that he will find Howard first so that I can get my paper signed before he has the chance to disappear again, or be disappeared by someone else."

"Your private detective, are you sure that he didn't find Howard already? When was the last time he checked in?"

"Last night. He hadn't found him yet. But he said that there are some rumors going around that he might have forced his way outside into the snow."

"Do you think he would do something like that?"

"Honestly, no. Howard hated to be cold. He would always bundle up when he had to go out in the snow and complain the entire time. I don't think, even drunk, that he would have gone outside knowing that he might not be able to get back in."

"Did you know that he'd been trying to stop drinking?"

"Sure. I knew. He sent me a long text, telling me he had changed, that he was sorry for everything that happened in our marriage, and he hoped I could forgive him." She frowned. "But obviously, he didn't stick to it."

"Did he text you often to apologize?"

"No, just that once. I almost believed him. I thought maybe when I found him, we would be able to hash some things out. But clearly, it was just another lie."

"Why do you say that?"

"I spoke to Ben, the bartender. He said that the last time he saw Howard he looked drunk. I'm guessing a bartender would know. Don't you think?"

"Yes, I suppose you're right about that."

"Anyway, if you're hoping to get any money out of him, good luck. As far as I know he's still broke. Do me a favor, if you find him first, let him know that I'm here and I'm looking for him."

"Sure, I will." Walt nodded to her, then turned and headed down the hall. Now that he'd spoken with Jennifer he doubted that she had the cruelty in her to kill Howard, but that didn't mean that she couldn't hire someone to do it. Maybe her private detective was more of a private assassin.

Chapter Thirteen

Jo walked towards the security office. It was nestled in the corner of the ground floor on the opposite side of the lobby. She'd noticed it the moment she entered the resort. It was well disguised with a few plants and a plain door, but she recognized its strategic position. When she opened the door she found a bank of screens and a security guard positioned in front of them.

"Excuse me, you can't be here." He stood up from his chair.

"I know, I'm sorry. I don't mean to interrupt, but I was wondering if Bart might be in?"

"He's in his office." He pointed to a door in the back of the room.

"Thanks." Jo knocked on the door then pushed it open. Bart sat behind his desk with his eyes on his computer.

"Bart, do you have a minute?"

He looked over at her with surprise, then glanced at his watch, then back at her. "Just."

"Great, that's all I need."

"Come on in." He stood up from his desk as she stepped into the office.

"Thanks for your time." She closed the door behind her. "As you know, my friends and I are very concerned about Howard."

"Yes, I understand that. However, I still think that Eddy was mistaken."

"Maybe so, but Howard is still missing, isn't he?"

"Yes, he is." He frowned.

"I've been told that Howard had an argument at dinner last night, with one of the other actors, Jeremiah. Do you know anything about that?"

"Any altercation is reported to security if it's witnessed by staff. So yes, I do know about the verbal argument that took place at dinner last night."

"Do you know what it was about?"

"Honestly, I haven't looked into it just yet. I have been focused on trying to assure everyone stirred up by last night's mistake, that no murder has taken place."

"Okay, forget about the murder theory. No matter what, Howard is missing. Don't you think that he would have turned up by now?"

He pursed his lips for a moment, then sat back down behind his desk. "Can you keep what I say between us?"

"Sure." Jo sat down across from him and met his eyes.

"We have reason to believe that Howard might have stumbled out into the snow. If he was drunk enough, he might have passed out. The truth is, we may not find Howard until after the snow begins to melt. It's a horrific thing to think, I know. I apologize if it upsets you, but it's the reality of living in a blizzard prone region. Sometimes missing people aren't found until the first thaw."

"But the snowstorm was pretty bad by the time Howard went missing."

"Yes, but as you said, he'd had an argument, maybe he was trying to get away."

"Did anyone on the wait staff hear what the argument was about?"

"I haven't talked to them, yet."

Jo shifted forward in her chair and rested her hands on Bart's desk. "Are you aware that there are some dangerous men in this resort?"

"What do you mean?"

"I mean, I overheard a conversation that involved threats of death, and criminal intent. Do you have a record of everyone who comes in and out of here?"

"Only if they reserve a room, or if the camera catches them."

"Did you review the camera feed?" Jo asked.

"I did. I don't see Howard leaving anywhere

on camera. But there are some places, such as the dining hall, that do not have cameras. The resort is quite expansive and not every exit can be covered."

"Do you run a check on everyone who works here?"

"Yes, I do." He studied her for a moment. "And some guests as well."

Jo's heart skipped a beat. With her criminal history she couldn't help but wonder if he was referring to her.

"Why would you run a check on a guest?"

"I like to know who is staying here." He shrugged.

"Anything interesting?"

"You could say that." He cleared his throat then glanced away from her. "Look, I don't usually share information about guests, but since you four are insisting on asking questions about this, you should know that the owner of a casino is staying here. He's quite a colorful character."

"Yes, the owner of Sheron's." She nodded. "We know about him already. Howard owed him some money?"

"Owes. He still owes him some money. Which is another reason why he might have dug his way out into the snow."

"What about a man named Carlisle? Do you know anything about him?"

"Carlisle." Bart's cheeks flushed. "Why do you ask?"

"Why don't you answer?" Jo looked into his eyes.

"Carlisle is a very dangerous man. I've dealt with him before because of Howard. As far as I know he is not in the resort."

"Well, you'd better start looking harder, because I know for a fact that he is."

"How?" Bart returned her gaze.

"I heard him threatening two men who are posing as resort employees. They were delivering room service."

"Are you certain about this?"

"Yes, and there was a third. I think he had a broken nose."

"How do you know so much about all of this? Do they know that you saw them?"

"No. They didn't see me. I was hiding."

"It sounds like a very odd story, but I will look into it."

"Please do. This Carlisle doesn't seem to be the type that pulls any punches. I think if Howard had a problem with him, then that might be why Howard's missing."

"I think that's a big assumption. I've yet to speak to anyone, besides the four of you, who doesn't think Howard just wandered off."

"So if he wandered off, he's dead under the snow, and if he didn't, he's dead inside this building. Either way you have a problem on your hands, Bart, and I think you're going to need to do something about it, don't you?"

"Yes, of course. Unfortunately, if you and your friends spread the details of this situation I think it may create panic, and as you're aware there's no way to leave the resort at this time. Are you interested in having mass panic while snowed in?"

"No, I'm not." Jo frowned.

"Neither am I. So forgive me if I am not ready to jump to the very big conclusion that Howard was actually killed rather than the unfortunate victim of a drunken mistake. Perhaps with your lifestyle you are more accustomed to intrigue and drama, but knowing Howard the way I do, I'm more inclined to assume he did make that drunken mistake."

"I'm not sure what you think you know about my lifestyle, but I can tell you that my friends and I are only here to offer you help, not to hinder. However, I do think that you should consider how it's going to look when the police begin a murder investigation and find out that you ignored the possibility that Howard was murdered, despite having an eye witness."

"All right. Enough." Bart stood up from his desk and walked over to the door. "When you come to me with more evidence of a crime, I will decide whether to treat this investigation as a missing person or a murder. If you want to play detective, then be a real detective, and gather some actual evidence."

"I thought that was your job?" She paused between Bart and the door as she looked him straight in the eye.

"My job is to maintain a peaceful and safe environment for the guests and staff of this resort. I believe I am doing that just fine."

"I see." Jo started to step through the door, but he leaned forward just enough to block her.

"I'm serious. If you do come across something, I'd like to be informed."

She turned her head to meet his eyes and

found there wasn't much distance between them. She thought about asking him about the staff who worked last night, but didn't think she would get any information out of him, and if he knew that she wanted to talk to the staff he might try to stop her. Walt had mentioned that there were staff rooms on the ground floor. After Bart's cold reaction she decided that she would try and talk to the staff first before asking Bart more about them.

"We'll keep you up to date." She ducked past him and out into the hallway. She didn't turn back until she heard the click of the door behind her. Then she paused and stared for a moment. Bart was a strange man. She couldn't help but wonder if he might have actually moved the body himself to protect the resort. He seemed to be very dedicated to his job, but even more dedicated to the owners than to the guests. Maybe he wanted to be informed, just so he could do damage control if they found anything. Jo shook her head as she walked down the hallway. She couldn't be distracted. There was too much at stake. She walked towards the staff rooms hoping that she might be able to find some staff who worked last night.

Chapter Fourteen

Eddy made his way to the bar. It was too early for it to be open, but the door was unlocked. When he stepped inside he noticed Ben behind the bar.

"Hey Ben, I need your help again, buddy."

"Oh?" He wiped a tall glass with a cloth and offered Eddy a sidelong look. "With what? The bar is not open yet."

"I was hoping you might be able to tell me a little bit about the other guests that are staying here."

"Shouldn't you know them better than me? They're your friends and neighbors right?"

"Not those guests. The other guests staying here."

"Hmm, okay." He set the glass down on the shelf behind the bar and turned to face him fully. "Why don't you just ask me directly whatever it is that you're getting at?"

"My friend almost had a run-in with some unsavory characters. She mentioned one went by the name of Carlisle."

"Carlisle?" He narrowed his eyes. "I didn't realize he was here. Where did she see him?"

"Near the bar."

"Huh." He picked up another glass and began to wipe it clean. "It's strange to me that he would be here, right when Howard goes missing."

"So, you know him?"

"Not personally, no. But I do know of him. He's a bit of a monster, to be honest."

"And now he's snowed in with all of us?"

"Well, the one good thing is that Carlisle keeps a low profile. Unless you've done something to upset him, he usually doesn't cause you any trouble."

"Do you think Howard had done anything to annoy him?"

"Sure. Carlisle is a loan shark, and Howard

has a tendency to deal with those types. He is probably mixed up with Carlisle. I'd say that's very likely."

"If that's the case, then could Carlisle be involved in his murder?"

"Disappearance." Ben set the glass down beside the first one. "You need to stop throwing that murder word around. You're going to get the wrong people upset."

"Are there people I should be afraid of upsetting?"

"Well for one, the group of actors that are about to put on the murder mystery. You're going to steal all of their thunder with your own murder mystery, aren't you?"

"I would think they would be concerned about their fellow actor."

"I would think that, too. But they know Howard well enough to be certain that he's off drunk somewhere."

"Even though he refused the drink that you

offered him?"

"Maybe he refused one, maybe someone was watching that he wanted to put on a show for, that doesn't mean he didn't binge drink later to make up for it. Trust me, I've seen it enough."

"Sounds like you were fed up with him."

"Not really." Ben sighed. "Honestly, it's a little complicated. I started working here pretty young, and Howard became a bit of a father figure to me. Not a great one, but you know, the closest thing to a father I've had."

"So, you two were close?"

"More like, we come to blows now and then. I try to keep him in line. But he's just a loose cannon. No one can ever predict what he's going to do next."

"What about Jeremiah? Do you know much about him?"

"He's new. A good kid, I guess. I mean, he takes his acting very seriously."

"Are there often new actors?"

"Actually, no. It's been the same crew for years. A few have come and gone, but very few."

"Why is that?" Eddy watched as Ben picked up the same glass he'd already cleaned, and began to clean it again.

"You know, once a crew has worked together so long, they become like a machine. I think it's just easier not to add new blood to the group. Plus, they're all very picky about who they will work with. Usually people aren't brought into the group unless there's some kind of personal connection to one of the actors."

"Did Jeremiah have a personal connection with any of the actors?"

"I'm not sure. From what I heard, no, but he did spend an awful lot of time with Howard."

"I noticed they argued at dinner. Do you know anything about that?"

"I heard something. Jeremiah was probably upset about Howard being drunk again. He was all about the performance. As soon as he arrived, Howard started acting like he was on this straight and narrow kick."

"Do you think Jeremiah would ever cause him any harm?" Eddy asked.

"No, I don't. I think the only person who caused Howard harm, was Howard. If there was anyone else out there that wanted to do damage to him they would have to wait in line, because Howard does a bang up job of it himself. Excuse me a second." Ben turned to another man behind the bar. "We're going to need a few blocks of ice for the lunch rush, can you bring them up front?"

"Sure." He stepped through the door that led to the storage room.

"Anything else I can do for you, Eddy?" Ben looked back at him.

"Do you think Jeremiah and Howard had some kind of history?"

"It's possible I guess. Now that I think about it, he could have invited Jeremiah. Since no one else claimed to, I guess he might have."

"If he did, why would he keep it under wraps?"

"I'm not sure, maybe Jeremiah didn't want to be associated with him."

"Thanks for the information, Ben. Just let me know if you overhear anyone talking about Howard. That would be very helpful."

"Sure, no problem. It's going to be a busy lunch, since the murder mystery starts this afternoon. I'll listen close."

"Thanks Ben." Eddy stood up and headed for the door of the bar. As he pushed it open he almost ran into a well-dressed man with two beautiful women, one on either side of him. He recognized him immediately as one of the men he had overheard on the third floor, when he had done his initial search. He could not see the other thick-set man so presumed he wasn't with him. "Excuse me."

"Did you get any service in there? That

bartender won't even give me a beer."

"I don't think he's allowed to serve before a certain time."

"I'm sure he lets the employees dip now and then. He wouldn't even take a bribe." He shook his head.

"Eddy." Eddy offered him his hand. "Are you here for the murder mystery?"

"Tad." He shook Eddy's hand. "No, I'm here for a mystery of my own. You haven't seen this guy around have you?" He held up his phone with a picture of Howard on it.

"No, sorry, not since yesterday."

"Oh, you did see him yesterday?"

"Sure, before dinner."

"But not after that?"

"No, I haven't seen him since." Eddy narrowed his eyes. "Except on the floor of the dining hall, dead."

"What?" Tad lowered his phone. "What are

you talking about?"

"Howard is dead. I saw it for myself."

"You're crazy. If Howard was dead, I would know about it."

"Someone moved the body. Someone, who didn't want to be caught."

"Look, I don't know what you're getting at here, but I don't like the tone of your voice. If you're going to accuse me of something, you ought to just come right out and say it," Tad growled.

"I know that you wanted Howard dead. Now he is." Eddy shoved his hands into his pockets and shrugged. "Is that a coincidence?"

"I had nothing to do with Howard going missing, or his death. As far as I know the little pipsqueak is still alive, and I hope that's the case, because I want my money."

"Howard is broke, you know that you're not going to get anything from him."

"No, he's not broke. I know for a fact that he

had a fifty thousand dollar windfall recently, that's why I'm here," Tad said.

"Where would he get that kind of money?" Eddy asked.

"An inheritance, I was told. Some distant relative died, and he was left the money. As soon as I heard about it I knew I had to collect, before he either gambled it away, or someone else came to collect. So no, I would not have killed Howard, that would defeat my purpose for being here, wouldn't it?"

"Yes, I guess it would, unless you got your money, and still wanted to get rid of him."

"That's a rather rude assertion to make. Do you think I'm a murderer?"

"I think things can get heated when there are large sums of money involved. Perhaps you lost control."

"No sir, I did nothing of the kind. I always get my money, but I am not a murderer. Now if you'll excuse me, I have more pressing matters to attend to." He pushed past Eddy. Eddy stared at him for a moment, then turned and walked away. If Howard really did have money, then things had changed again. If Carlisle and Jennifer also knew about the money, then either of them could have been driven to kill in an attempt to get it.

Chapter Fifteen

As Jo walked down the hallway, away from the security room her attention was caught by a couple of staff members going into a room. She walked towards the room, but the door was closed. She could hear laughter from inside. She knocked on the door. When a young woman opened it, she was surprised to see several people around her. For a small guest room, there were quite a few staff members crammed inside.

"Hi, do you have a minute?" Jo smiled at the woman who opened the door.

"A minute for what? We're not on shift until lunch. If you need something you can call down to the front desk."

"Oh no, I don't need anything. I just wanted a chance to talk with all of you, if that's okay?" She smiled at the other staff members in the room.

"Talk to us about what?" One of the young men glanced at the others in the room. "What's this about?"

"I was just wondering if you might be able to answer a few questions for me."

"We're not involved in the murder mystery."

"It's not about the murder mystery. It's about one of the actors, Howard. Did you know him?"

"Howard? Sure we all do. He's a trip." The young man laughed. "It's hard not to miss him."

"Is he? How so?"

"Oh well, he's always getting himself into some kind of trouble. I guess you could say he's the comic relief around here."

"Only when he's drunk. He's hilarious." A woman seated on the couch laughed. "If you ever need cheering up just give Howard a drink."

"What about last night at dinner? He didn't seem very funny then."

"No, he wasn't." She frowned. "He got into it with Jeremiah, and he knows better. I told him to get out before Bart got hold of him."

"Oh, what would Bart do if he got hold of him?"

"Bart has his ways." The first man she spoke with rolled his eyes. "He doesn't fire people, he just coerces them into doing what he wants."

"Is he always so strict?" Jo asked.

"Bart's all right. He helped me out when one of the guests was harassing me." Another woman stood up. "And yes, he has to keep Howard in line, because when he's drunk he does stupid things. Jeremiah shouldn't have said those things to him though."

"What did Jeremiah say?" Jo met her eyes.

"He told him that he was a worthless drunk, and that he had ruined everything. That he didn't deserve to be alive. He said something about how he shouldn't have invited him here if he wasn't going to change."

"Howard shouldn't have invited Jeremiah?"

"Yeah, that's right. I thought that was a little strange because I didn't think they even knew

180

each other, but that's what he said." She shrugged. "Anyway, if Jeremiah knew anything about Howard he'd know better than to talk to him like that. Howard doesn't like to be yelled at. He's usually a happy drunk, but if he gets angry, you don't want to be around him."

"Have you heard any chatter about guests looking for Howard?"

"Well." One of the young men hesitated as he spoke. He ran his hands over his knees and frowned. "Everyone knows that Tad Billings and his ex-wife are here because of him."

"Word gets around?"

"Yeah, especially since Tad Billings offered a reward to any staff member that could find Howard and bring him to his room."

"What?" Jo's eyes widened. "Did anyone find him?"

"No, of course not. Bart got wind of the offer and he warned all of us that if we do anything to help Tad, we're going to lose our jobs and possibly face arrest." He shook his head. "I don't know if he can really arrest anyone for that, but if there is a way Bart will find it."

"It sounds to me like Bart is very protective of Howard."

"He's protective of everyone here." One of the women nodded. "He looks out for us. If we get out of line, we know it, but he'd rather retain his employees than hire new ones."

"The owner of the resort pretty much lets Bart run the place?" Jo asked.

"Yes. I don't think he really reports to anyone."

"Interesting. So he'd have a lot to lose if something bad happened here?"

"Maybe." The woman glanced at her watch. "We're running out of time before lunch."

"All right, thanks for your time everyone. If you think of anything, and you want to reach out." She offered a card with her name and number to the woman who answered the door. "Please feel free to contact me."

"No reward?" The young man behind her asked.

"I wouldn't want to upset Bart." Jo winked, then left the room. As she headed down the hallway she decided to take the stairs up to the second floor. As she started walking up the stairs she heard the scuff of a shoe behind her. She turned around to see a man on the landing behind her. It took her a moment, but she recognized him as Bart.

"Were you following me?" She stared down at him.

"Shouldn't I be?" He looked up at her with a frown. "You're determined to put yourself in danger."

"I haven't done anything wrong."

"Maybe not, but be aware, I have my eye on you."

"Thanks, I'm aware. I think I'll take the elevator." She climbed the last few steps to the first floor and ducked into the hallway. She tried to shake off the uneasiness he left her with as she pressed the button for the elevator. She wasn't sure if he was being considerate, controlling, or downright creepy. When she reached the room, Eddy, Samantha, and Walt had just arrived.

"Walt, did you find any record of an inheritance in Howard's financial history? I was told by Tad Billings that he had a recent windfall." Eddy sat down at the table beside him.

"No, but maybe I missed it if it was a small amount."

"It wasn't. It was a large amount. Fifty thousand"

"Wow! Hmm, no I didn't see anything, but I'll look it back over again. I don't think I could have missed something like that though. Maybe he kept it in cash somehow," Walt said.

"If he had money like that, then there is even more motive for everyone who came here to collect."

"But if he had the money, why wouldn't he have paid off some of his debts?" Samantha asked.

"It wouldn't have even covered half of it," Walt said.

"Maybe he was trying to hide the money to give himself something to survive on." Eddy scratched the back of his neck. "That could really cause some anger in those that he owed money to."

"I think we should consider Bart as well. He's very involved with Howard, and highly protective of his position here at the resort. I think he might have been up to something. Not only that, but I found out that Howard is the one who invited Jeremiah here," Jo said.

"Oh really, Ben mentioned that might be the case. I think we need to have another conversation with Jeremiah."

"Yes, I agree. But we're getting tight on time." Jo glanced at her watch, then frowned. "The murder mystery is going to start in about an hour."

"Good, that means that Jeremiah should be heading down to the lobby soon." Eddy stood up. "Let's see if we can catch him before he gets there. Walt, do you know which floor Jeremiah is staying on?"

"Uh, I think all of the actors are on the third floor. But let me just confirm that." He clicked through a few screens on his computer, then nodded. "He should be on the third floor."

"Good, let's head up there and wait for him by the elevator. We can act like we just happened to be there, and it will be less confrontational."

"Good idea, but I don't think we should all go, Eddy. Just you and Sam," Jo said.

"You think?" Samantha looked up.

"You two make a good team. Eddy gets to the point and you can keep people calm, Sam. I'll stay here with Walt and keep digging into things."

"All right, let's go now before we miss him."

Eddy and Samantha stepped out of the room and headed to the third floor. When they stepped off the elevator the hallway was empty.

"It seems like Jo is really getting suspicious of Bart."

"I don't blame her. He acts strange."

"Who doesn't in this place?" Samantha sighed. "I'm not sure we're ever going to figure this one out."

"Don't give up, we're getting close, I can feel it." Eddy tilted his head towards a door that opened at the end of the hallway.

"Here he comes. Pretend we don't see him," Samantha suggested.

"All right. I guess I just said something very interesting."

"Yes, you did. I'm very interested. I'm not even paying attention to the man walking down the corridor towards us."

"How close is he?"

"Just seconds now, and go."

Eddy turned to face Jeremiah. "Ah, Jeremiah, it's good to see you again."

"I don't have time to talk, I need to get down to the lobby."

"Well, we just have one question for you."

"No, no more questions." He looked between Eddy and Samantha with red-rimmed eyes. "I have nothing more to say." He started to push past him, but Eddy blocked his way.

"It's time to tell the truth, Jeremiah. I know that Howard invited you here. So how did you really know him? There's much more to this story than you're telling."

"It's none of your business." He scowled as he stepped around Eddy in an attempt to get to the elevator.

"Wait just a minute." Eddy placed his hand over the elevator call button. "It is our business. A man is dead."

"He's not dead. He's missing. Because he went off and got drunk again. Now let me pass before I call security."

"He is dead. I'm sorry to tell you this, Jeremiah, but he is very much dead. I saw him with my own eyes, I checked for a pulse, and I know for a fact that he is dead."

Jeremiah looked over at him. For just a moment his expression flickered with shock.

"That's not true. You're just trying to upset me."

"Would that upset you? How did you know Howard?"

"You're sick, you know that? You come here for the murder mystery, but the show isn't enough? You have to invent a crime and try to rub it in everyone's faces? There's nothing normal about that."

"Jeremiah." Eddy stared hard into his eyes. "I'm not inventing anything. I can tell that you cared about Howard, and you should know the truth. He's dead. I'm sorry."

"You're wrong." Jeremiah shook his head. "It can't be true. Move." He pushed Eddy's hand out of the way of the button and pressed it in. "I have nothing else to say to you." The elevator doors slid open, and he stepped inside. "If you cause me any more trouble I will go to the resort security and file harassment charges. I need to get in character, not to be hassled by you." The elevator doors slid shut again. Eddy looked over at Samantha.

"I guess we're not going to get much more out of him."

"Fine, if he's not going to tell us, then we're going to find out for ourselves. Let's go." Eddy pushed open the door to the stairwell and they climbed back down to the second floor.

Once inside the room again, he fixed his gaze on Walt.

"All right, that's it, we need to figure out what Jeremiah's connection to Howard is. It is obviously more than just a friendship, or even

Jeremiah having a problem with Howard's professional behavior."

"I agree." Walt nodded. "I think Howard has a lot of secrets that we haven't dug up yet. I'm going to go back through his life year by year and see what changes and moves he made. Maybe there's something there that will give us some insight into Jeremiah's relationship with him."

"Okay Walt, good idea. While you do that, I'm going to see if I can get some more information on Tad Billings, from the people he keeps closest, his girlfriends. Sam, maybe you should come with me."

"Me? Why? I was going to help Walt with the search for information on Jeremiah."

"Because, I need a woman there. I don't want those girls to get the wrong impression."

"You mean you're afraid you might be distracted by their beauty?" Samantha smiled.

"I didn't say that at all." Eddy shrugged.

"Okay, I'll tag along."

"I'm going to find out where Carlisle is hiding. He hasn't made any appearances since the first time I overheard him in the storage room. If he's laying that low it might be because he knows that Howard's body could be found at any moment." Jo narrowed her eyes. "Plus, I don't feel safe with him roaming the resort."

"Use extra caution, Jo, we know what Carlisle is capable of, and if he feels threatened he will come out swinging." Walt caught her arm and met her eyes. "No one needs to be a hero here, Howard is already dead."

"I hear you, Walt, I promise." Jo turned and left the room.

"Don't worry, Walt, Jo will be careful. Let's go, Eddy, before it gets too close to the start of the murder mystery."

"All right. Let us know what you find, Walt." Eddy tipped his hat to Walt, then held the door open for Samantha.

Chapter Sixteen

Walt stared at his computer for a moment. The kind of research he intended to do would normally take him quite some time. He wanted to get it done as fast as possible. Instead of going year by year, he decided to start with major life changes. First, when Howard moved out of his childhood home, then when he got married, and finally when he got divorced. Each life event could put enough pressure on him to make him change direction, or get involved with someone new. Walt dug into the information on the house Howard grew up in, when it was purchased, when it was sold. His father struggled to keep ownership of the house, and sold it when Howard was fourteen. He died five years later, in a car accident. Howard was on his own at a young age, and his troubles began early as well. He had a record for petty theft, and disorderly conduct. He was arrested with another young man, Dan Baxter. A quick check confirmed that Dan Baxter attended the same high school as Howard, and was the same age. Walt assumed they were friends. This was confirmed when Howard's first apartment was co-leased with Dan. Dan was on record as a witness at Howard's wedding.

Howard and Dan also opened a business together, a car lot, about five years into Howard's marriage. The car lot only lasted about two years. He looked into why it shut down and discovered a financial mess.

Walt sighed and skimmed through the employee list to see if Jeremiah might be one of them. Jeremiah was young, but he could have been eighteen when the business failed. However, he wasn't listed on any business records. So far he hadn't found a single trace of a connection with Jeremiah. As Walt's frustration built he decided to take a walk. Moving, and changing environments helped him to clear his mind and come up with new ideas. As he made his way down the hall he noticed one of the doors was open. It only took him a moment to surmise that it was room 217.

"That's it, I'm done. I'm not paying you a single dime more if you can't bring me more information than that."

"I did find out something."

"Something that is completely useless to me. What do I care if Howard had a love child? He and I had a terrible marriage. It doesn't surprise me in the least that he would have knocked boots with someone else, or that he would have been a dead beat to his own child."

"Still, it might lead to Howard."

"How?"

"His son is here, in this resort."

"And?"

"And maybe he's the reason that his father is missing."

"You think he might have killed Howard?"

"According to one eyewitness Howard is dead. Now, the guy could be a nut job, but I looked into him. He's a retired cop with no reason to make up a story. I'm more inclined to believe it now that I know Howard had so many enemies here. Between the casino owner, the loan shark, and you, I can't believe that no one has found him yet."

"I can't believe that I ever paid you a dime. You're done, you're fired."

"You can't fire me because your ex-husband is missing."

"You're a private detective, you're supposed to be detecting. Since you're not, yes, I absolutely can fire you. As soon as this dreadful snow melts, I am putting Howard in my rear view mirror and leaving him there. I don't care what you do, but I don't want to see you again, understand?"

"Sure, I understand. Just remember, no refunds."

"Yeah, yeah. Just more money wasted on that fool, now get out."

Walt ducked to the other side of the hallway

as the detective stepped out. If the man noticed him, he didn't offer a signal that he did. Walt had to question his merit as a detective since his observation skills were not great. The door to 217 slammed shut. The sharp sound jolted Walt into action. Someone at the resort was Howard's son, which meant someone had a lot more at stake than they claimed. He hurried back to the room and settled at the computer again. Now he had a new direction to search in.

***

Samantha and Eddy stood just inside the bar. Tad was certainly there, with his entourage, and in a demanding mood.

"How are we going to get them away from him?" Eddy frowned as he watched Tad at the bar. It had just opened for drinks before the murder mystery would start, and of course Tad was first in line. His two girlfriends flanked him.

"Allow me." Samantha smiled and walked towards the group. Eddy hung back near the door, and did his best to blend in with the wall. Samantha reached the bar and leaned her elbows against the top of it. She glanced over at the woman right beside her.

"Hi, I'm Samantha."

"Hi." The woman stared at her.

"Are you here for the murder mystery?" Samantha asked.

"The what?" She shook her head. "No. I'm just here to keep my honey company."

"That's right." Tad looked over at Samantha. "Is there something you want?"

"Sorry to bother you all, I just wondered if you might be able to help me."

"Help you what?" Tad narrowed his eyes.

"I seem to have lost my date."

"Your date?" Tad chuckled. "How are we supposed to help with that?"

"He said he was coming to the bar. But he's not here. I thought maybe you've seen him?" She displayed the picture of Howard on her phone. "He said he'd meet me here."

"That's your date?" Tad stood up.

"Yes, do you know him? Was he in here?"

"Oh yes, I know him. Where did you see him last?"

"Well, that's what I'm asking you."

"Don't get smart with me." Tad scowled at her and stood so close that Samantha had to lean back to get some breathing room. "You tell me where he is, right now."

"I have no idea, that's why I'm asking you. He said he was going up to his room on the third floor, and then would meet me at the bar."

"What room? Did he say what room?"

"I think it was 305." She shrugged. "I'm not sure though. I'm not the type of woman to go up to some random man's room, even if he did take me to an expensive dinner a few nights ago."

"Oh really? He took you to an expensive

dinner? With my money?" Tad's hands balled into fists. "I'm going to find him for you, right now. You two, stay with her, don't let her out of your sight." He turned and stormed out of the bar. Samantha winked at Eddy and waved him over.

"Hello ladies." Eddy smiled at them as he leaned on the bar beside them. "Do you have a minute to chat?"

"I guess, Tad told us not to go anywhere."

"Have either of you seen Tad with this man? Howard?" Samantha showed them the picture again.

"Your date? No." The woman closest to Samantha shook her head. "I know he's looking for him though. He owes Tad a lot of money."

"I did hear him talking about Howard though with that creepy guy, Carlisle." The woman beside Eddy nodded.

"You met Carlisle?" Samantha raised an eyebrow.

"Yes, he and Tad were in the room talking last

night. Carlisle came in with a couple of guys and started threatening Tad to stay away from his payday. Then Tad started yelling at Carlisle that Howard owed him money first, and he had first dibs on him."

"Really?" Eddy frowned. "Did either of them mention Howard being gone, or hurt, or even dead?"

"No. In fact, Carlisle agreed that when he found him, he would bring Howard to Tad and they could both have some fun with him." She shook her head. "I don't like that kind of talk. Tad's not usually violent, but he is pretty mad at this Howard guy." She lowered her voice. "I hope he doesn't find him. I don't know what he'll do to him."

"It's all right, don't worry. He won't find him." Samantha sighed and looked over at Eddy. "I guess we've hit another dead end."

As they walked back to the room, Samantha and Eddy discussed their suspects.

"It seems to me that we're the only ones that know for sure that Howard is dead. If that's the case, then who killed him? One of them has to know that he's dead," Samantha said.

"Or they're just putting on a show. At this point, if one of these people did kill Howard, the rest are going to be very angry that they didn't get their chance to collect from him. So whoever killed him might just be pretending they don't know he's dead."

"That's true, but if so, they're doing a pretty good job of it. Maybe the murder mystery actors aren't the only great talents around here."

"Criminals do tend to be very good at deceit and lying."

"Good point." Samantha pushed the button for the elevator and they both stepped inside.

Chapter Seventeen

Jo lingered near the back entrance of the resort. It was used for deliveries, and equipment. If she wanted to sneak in and out of the resort, or find a quiet place to discuss matters the delivery entrance was where she would go. Since there was no chance of anything getting delivered due to the blizzard outside, it was an even better place to lay low. After several minutes slipped by, she wondered if she'd made the right call. She was just about to give up and head back to the room, when she heard footsteps approaching. The closer they came, the more anxious she became. There were plenty of places to hide, but she didn't want to hide this time. Surprising a man like Carlisle, would only lead to bad things.

"I think he's lying to me. He's got to know where Howard is. I don't want this guy leaving here with him. I want my hands on Howard, understand?"

"Yes, I understand, Chief, but what if Tad doesn't have him? I haven't been able to find anything that indicates he does."

"Howard has to be here somewhere. He's either hiding really well, or someone has him."

"There's only so many places, Chief. We've looked everywhere."

"No, you haven't!" Carlisle's voice raised so suddenly and fiercely that Jo jumped. "If you looked everywhere, then you would have found him!"

"Chief, security thinks he might have wandered out in the blizzard."

"Then you go out in the snow and you find his body, because until you bring him to me, you haven't done your job, and I don't want to hear another excuse from you. If I leave here without Howard, I can tell you right now, there are going to be consequences."

"Chief, we're trying..."

Jo cringed at the sound of skin striking skin.

"I said, no more excuses. Get out of my sight before I decide to make an example out of you."

Jo stood her ground as she heard one set of retreating footsteps, and another approaching her. When Carlisle rounded the corner he stopped, and stared at her.

"Who are you?"

"I'm part of the murder mystery. I'm supposed to be here. Who are you?"

"Clear out of here, there's no need for you to be here," Carlisle demanded.

"I can be wherever I choose. You're a guest, you shouldn't be down here."

"Watch your tone." He stepped closer to her. "You have no idea who you're dealing with."

"Just another guest at a resort, right? Unless there's something else I should know?"

"That depends on whether you're going to cause me any trouble."

"I was going to ask you the same question." Jo

crossed her arms and studied him. "I heard the way you were talking to that guy. You think you're some kind of tough guy?"

"I don't have to think it." He chuckled. "But apparently you think you're something yourself. What's with the attitude?"

"I just don't like to hear people get pushed around."

"Why not? If he did his job, I wouldn't have to push him around."

"Maybe it's an impossible job. Maybe you know that."

"What are you talking about?"

"I know who you are, Mr. Carlisle. I know who you're looking for."

"Ah, so you're not as ignorant as you claim. Then you should know better than to speak to me like this. Alone?" He glanced around the open concrete room. "Do you really think that's wise?"

"I'm not afraid of you, Carlisle. I've dealt with

men like you many times before."

"Men like me?" He chuckled. "I doubt that."

"Feel free to underestimate me, it doesn't usually end well."

"What do you want from me?"

"I know that Howard is dead. What I don't understand, is why did you kill him?"

"What do you mean why did I kill him? I didn't kill him. He's not dead, as far as I know."

"He is. But if he owed you money, why would you kill him instead of trying to get the money from him?"

"Howard doesn't have any money. But yes, he still owes me, and I will find a way to collect."

"You know something about him, don't you?" Jo stared into his eyes. "What do you have on him?"

"Listen, I have no idea who you are, but you're not going to question me. I don't have to tell you anything."

"No you don't, but I know for a fact that Howard is dead. So either you can believe me and ask me how I know that, or you can just keep chasing a ghost, hoping for a shakedown."

"You know an awful lot for an actress."

"You know very little for someone who thinks he knows everything."

"There's that mouth again." He laughed. "I think I could enjoy your company."

"So, what do you know?"

"I know that Howard did have something to lose."

"What's that?"

"His son."

"His what? Howard didn't have any children."

"Oh, so there's something that you don't know? Surprise, surprise. Yes, Howard does have a son, and the moment I get my hands on Howard he's going to find a way to get me my money, or his son is going to pay the price. So if you see our dear old dead Howard, please pass on that message to him. Until then, you need to stay out of my business." He pointed his finger directly at Jo. "Or you'll face your own consequences." He turned and walked away. Jo stared after him, still stunned by his revelation. Was it bad information, or could he be right? She took the elevator back to the second floor. When she reached the room, she opened it to find Walt, Eddy, and Samantha, gathered around Walt's computer.

"Does anyone know if Howard had a son?"

"We're looking into that right now." Eddy frowned as he straightened up. "How did you find out about it?"

"Apparently, Carlisle knows about it, and knows who he is. He was going to use Howard's son as leverage to get whatever he could out of Howard."

"Howard also had some money. I was able to confirm that he did receive an inheritance that he never put in any account that I can find," Walt said.

"That's funny." Jo shook her head.

"Funny?" Samantha looked up at her. "Why?"

"Howard lived his life broke and in debt, but he died a wealthy man."

"Wealthy might be pushing it." Walt shook his head.

"He had a lot more than he ever had when he was alive," Samantha said.

"That I can agree with."

"So, did you find his son?" Jo walked over to the table to join them.

"No, not yet. We've been looking at all of the possibilities. So far only a few people come up as potential children. We've assumed that Howard's son is here at the resort. So we're checking employees and guests. We've only come across six that match the age range."

"Anyone we know?"

"Two actually." Walt turned the screen so Jo

could see. "Jeremiah, and Ben."

"The bartender?" Jo tilted her head to the side as she surveyed the faces of both men. She brought up the picture of Howard on her phone and tried to compare their features. "Either one of them could pass for his son."

"So could the rest. Without having an idea of who the mother is, we really can't base too much on genetics, given that none of them looks especially like Howard," Walt said.

"It would certainly explain Jeremiah's connection with Howard. And the fact that Howard invited him to the resort," Jo said.

"Maybe, but if Jeremiah was his son, why wouldn't he tell us?" Eddy asked.

"Maybe, he didn't know. Or maybe, he killed Howard when he found out." Jo sighed. "Having an absent parent suddenly come into your life could be traumatic enough to cause a rash reaction."

"What about Ben though?" Eddy tapped the

face on the screen.

"Don't touch!" Walt grimaced.

"Sorry. But Ben seems to know an awful lot about Howard."

"And again, if he knew he was Howard's son, he didn't tell us." Jo pursed her lips. "We have a bigger problem, too."

"What's that?" Samantha glanced away from the screen.

"As long as Carlisle believes that Howard is alive, whoever is actually Howard's son, is in danger. Carlisle might get desperate and grab him, or hurt him in some way."

"Then we need to find out who he is. We know that Jeremiah has a connection with Howard, and Ben knows quite a bit about him. I guess the best we can do is ask each of them," Eddy said.

"But what if they don't know?" Walt looked between his friends. "Maybe Howard never had the chance to tell them. I think our best bet is to see if we can find the mother. If we connect the mother to Howard, then we should be able to find the son."

"All right, but the murder mystery is going to begin soon, and we need to be there," Samantha said.

"You three head down, I'm going to keep doing some research. If I figure out who Howard's son is, I'll text you," Walt said.

"Okay, Sam, you and Jo go ahead. There's something I want to check on, then I will meet you at the café," Eddy said.

"Okay, see you there." Jo held the door for Samantha. They walked down the hallway to the elevator in silence.

"Are you okay, Sam?"

"I don't know. I guess, it was easier to think of Howard just as some drunken gambler with no one to miss him. Now that I know he had a son, it makes things more real I guess."

"Yes, I wonder if his son even had the chance to meet him." Jo frowned. "Some secrets we carry, aren't meant to be buried with us."

In the elevator on the way down to the lobby, Jo took a call. She excused herself as she stepped out of the elevator. Samantha walked over to the front wall of the lobby. It had been some time since she actually looked out the window. The blanket of white that covered everything she could see dazzled her. In just hours, the entire landscape around the resort had been transformed. Even though it was daylight, the sky was dark with heavy clouds. Snow swirled past the glass in a constant barrage of mystical white flakes. It was beautiful, but also intimidating. Already, the snow was piled up to the base of the windows, and with the speed of the snowfall it appeared it would continue to pile even higher. When she stepped closer to the window she could hear the wind howl past. It wasn't just an ordinary snowfall. It was a fierce storm, prepared to bring the entire area to its knees.

"Beautiful, isn't it?" Jo stepped up beside her.

"Yes, it is." Samantha frowned. "But also a

little frightening. I don't think I've ever seen so much snow."

"Don't worry, it's supposed to stop in the next hour or two, then the plows will get to work."

"I guess we might not be staying that extra day."

"It depends on how much progress the plows are able to make. Some of the roads we took in may take a while for the plows to clear."

"Do you think that Howard could be out there?" Samantha's eyes widened.

"What do you mean? You believe he might have gotten drunk and wandered out?"

"No, but maybe the killer had time to hide his body out there somewhere. If so, then we may never find the body. Or at least not for a long time. Any evidence will be ruined by the snow."

"It's a possibility, but I'm hoping that's not the case. It makes me uneasy to think that we're trapped here with a murderer. The closer we get to finding Howard's body, the more nervous the murderer is going to be," Jo commented.

"I agree. At any moment the murderer could panic and decide to do something rash. Is Bart any closer to helping us with this?"

"He's still claiming that Howard was just drunk, that there never was a murder, so no."

"Okay, then we're going to have to ramp up our investigation. I think we should talk to Jennifer again. It's just too convenient that she showed up now, and she had the motive of missing money, and bitterness for the failed marriage. Everyone else we suspect was just out for money. Killing Howard wouldn't get them that."

"That's true. But if they knew he didn't have the money to pay back, they might have decided to use him as an example."

"Then why hide the body? Wouldn't they want the murder to be known?"

"Maybe they realized that they had no way out and they hid the body to try to protect themselves."

"Maybe." Samantha shook her head. "Something just feels like it's missing here. Poor guy had more targets on him than anyone I've ever known."

"A lifetime of mistakes can certainly lead to that."

"Let's head to the café, that's where the murder mystery starts. Eddy is waiting to regroup with us there and plan out our next steps."

"All right. Any news from Walt on Howard's son?"

"No, not yet. Maybe Eddy knows something."

Jo led the way to the café, where Eddy and several other people were gathered waiting for the murder mystery to start.

"Any news, Eddy?" Samantha sat down beside him.

"Walt said he's found a woman that Howard saw a few times, and right now he's tracking down whether she had any children. We should know something soon. I think the best idea is for us to just play along with the murder mystery. That will give the impression to anyone observing that we've given up on the real murder mystery. Maybe someone will let their guard down."

"Okay, you two solve the mystery. I'm going to go check out the storage room by the dining hall again. If Carlisle did have something to do with this then he might have used that room to stash the body somehow," Jo said.

"All right, be careful." Samantha met her eyes. "Make sure that you check in with us before you go anywhere else."

"I will. You and Eddy make sure that you win that cruise, and keep an eye on anyone acting suspicious."

"Will do." Eddy nodded. "As Sam said, be careful."

Chapter Eighteen

Jo walked off towards the bar as her friends stayed at the café. She wondered if Carlisle would tolerate another run-in with her. This time she planned to avoid being seen by him. When she neared the bar she noticed that the camera that usually pointed to the door had been turned away from it. Her heartbeat quickened, she had put the camera back in its original position so someone had to have moved it. Which meant that someone was up to something. She slipped into the bar, which was empty, then into the storage room. As quietly as she could she backed into the shadows and surveyed the room. Maybe someone was in there with her, already hiding. After a few minutes of silence she decided that there was no one else there. She began to look through the storage area, then crossed over into the kitchen section. One of the large freezers had an out of order sign on it. She stared at it for a long moment. If she wanted to hide a body, somewhere that no one would see or smell it, a freezer would be a good option.

An out of order freezer would be the best idea. If it wasn't actually broken. She walked over to the freezer and placed her hand on the side of it. Right away she felt her skin cool. If the freezer was out of order, why was it still plugged in? Why was it still so cold? She bit into her bottom lip as she reached for the handle. When she opened the door there would either be a body or a lot of spoiled meat. She wasn't sure which she preferred. A part of her still held on to a small sense of hope that Howard might be alive.

Jo tugged at the handle until the door swung open. Right away she was hit with a blast of cold air. There was no way the freezer wasn't doing its job. The space beyond the door was just large enough to be considered a walk-in freezer. There were several large blocks of ice, but no food. She inched a little further in, while trying to make sure that the door stayed open behind her. Beyond a few blocks of ice she noticed something much darker. Her stomach twisted as she realized it was a bedspread identical to the one she'd slept under the night before. Why would anyone put a bedspread in a freezer? They wouldn't.

Jo took a deep breath and stepped all the way into the freezer. It was easy to see that there was something hidden beneath the bedspread. She grabbed the corner of it, and tugged. But the bedspread was frozen to the floor, and to whatever was under it. She tugged again, and this time it was hard enough to discover a pair of shoes under the bedspread. Her stomach churned again as she noted the feet that were tucked into the shoes. This was definitely a dead body. This was definitely Howard.

"Jo?" The voice echoed from the entrance of the storage area. She recognized it right away as Bart's. Had he stashed the body in here to hide it? What would he do if he found out that she discovered it? Her heart raced as she backed out of the freezer. She pushed the door closed and turned to face Bart just as he walked up to her. "What are you doing in here?"

"How did you know I was here?"

"I saw you on the camera. I wanted to see what you were up to."

"Well, that's a little unsettling. Are you watching me now?"

"I just wanted to be sure you were safe." He reached out to take her hand, and gasped when his fingertips grazed it. "You're so cold. Were you outside?"

"No, I just, uh. I was looking for some ice cream. You know, stress eating."

"Ah." He nodded. "I'm very familiar with that myself. Here, let me show you where the chef hides his stash. It's the best Dutch chocolate you'll ever taste."

"That's okay, I think my sweet tooth has passed. I'm just going to head up to my room."

"All right. Are you sure you're okay? Did something happen?"

"No, nothing. It just hit me that I'm not really

hungry, I'm just tired."

"I'll walk you up."

"Great, that would be nice." As they left the storage room she glanced back over her shoulder for just a moment. Now that she knew where Howard was, the question was, who else did? If Bart knew the body was there, he was hiding it well. She was tempted to tell him what she found, but she couldn't be sure if she could trust him. In the elevator on the way to the second floor, she rubbed her hands together to warm them.

"I know you're up to something, Jo. Whatever it is, I can help you if you need it. You don't need to see me as your enemy."

"I don't."

"Then, what were you really doing in the storage room?" He looked into her eyes.

"Like I said, I wanted a snack."

He reached over and pushed the emergency stop button on the elevator. Her heart jumped up into her throat. Maybe he knew what she found.

Maybe he was the one who put Howard in the freezer.

"Why don't you start telling me the truth? Is it because you don't trust anyone in a position of authority?"

"Excuse me? What are you talking about?"

"I'm talking about the update that you and your friends promised me. I know that you're on to something. I want to know what it is."

"Why? According to you Howard's out there somewhere under a snow drift."

"Maybe I have reason to believe otherwise now."

"What reason?" She studied him.

"Is there a reason you're holding back information? You keep looking at me as if I've done something wrong."

"I don't know. Have you? Maybe you wanted to protect the reputation of the resort no matter what it took to do that?"

"I can't believe that you would even consider that."

"Why not?" She stood her ground as he took a step towards her.

"You think I'm a murderer?"

"Maybe not. Maybe you just hid Howard's body to protect the resort."

"Wow!" He stared at her, then turned and restarted the elevator. "Never mind. I can handle the investigation on my own. Obviously, you've decided who I am based on a short time of knowing me. On the other hand, I know that you've committed crimes in the past, and yet, I didn't assume that you were still a criminal. So which of us should be trusted?" The elevator lurched into motion. Jo grabbed on to the railing and watched him as he stared hard at the elevator doors. Had she misjudged him?

"All I'm trying to do is find out what happened to Howard. What new information do you have?"

"Like I said, if I'm on my own, then so are

you." He stepped off the elevator and headed down the hallway. She stepped off the elevator and followed after him.

"Bart wait."

"What is it?" He looked over his shoulder. "Are you ready to tell me the truth?"

"The plows are going to be here soon, and then we'll be leaving. Are you just going to pretend that Howard wasn't killed? Are you going to tell the police to investigate a murder, or a missing person?"

"That's entirely up to the evidence, isn't it?" He stared hard into her eyes. "Unless you have anything new to add, I can only assume that Howard is missing. I'm sorry if that disappoints you."

"That's all I need to know." She started to walk towards her room, when she turned around and saw that Bart was no longer in sight she walked towards the stairs instead. She walked back down the stairs to the lobby. If he wasn't willing to even consider the idea that Howard was dead, then she didn't trust him. Any good security officer, or detective, would at least consider it. At least, she thought they would. In the hallway on the way to the lobby she caught sight of Eddy as he stepped out of the stairwell.

"Eddy! Over here." Jo waved to him as she approached him.

"Jo, what is it? Did you find something?"

"Yes, I did, sh." She glanced over her shoulder to be sure no one was close enough to hear her. "I found him." She tugged on his arm until he was away from a woman who hurried towards the lobby, most likely to catch the tail end of the murder mystery.

"What do you mean?"

"I found Howard."

"Are you kidding?"

"No. He's in a freezer in the storage room behind the bar." She shuddered at the memory. "It has a sign on it that says out of order. No one would have bothered to look in there. I decided to take a peek and I found him, very much dead."

"This is great news, well I mean, not great news, but at least we know what happened to him now."

"No, we really don't. All we know is where he is. How are we going to find out who put him there?"

"Have you told anyone about finding the body?" Eddy asked.

"No, just you. But Bart suspects something. I was afraid to tell him, in case he's the one who put Howard there."

"Now that we know where Howard's body is hidden we can hopefully use that to figure out who killed him."

"The freezer is in the same room I was in when Carlisle and his goons were arguing," Jo said.

"They could have stashed the body there."

"Yes, it's possible, but when I spoke with Carlisle he seemed to be genuinely surprised at the thought of Howard being dead."

"That can be faked, easily."

"You're right."

"Let's gather everyone and see if we can get to the bottom of this," Eddy suggested.

"Where's Sam?"

"She is still solving the murder mystery, I went to snoop around while most of the people were preoccupied with the mystery."

"All right, I'll grab Samantha and Walt. Where are we going to meet?"

"Your room?" Eddy suggested.

"No, there's cameras everywhere. If Bart suspects that we know something he will likely be watching where we go. I think he said one of the few places that doesn't have a camera is the dining hall. It's still too early for dinner so it should be empty. Let's meet there."

"Okay, I'm going to check on the body and make sure it's still there."

"Eddy, do you think that's a good idea? What if someone sees you?"

"Did you get any pictures of the body?"

"No, I didn't. Bart was right outside, so I had to hurry."

"I understand, but I need some pictures of Howard's body in case whoever put him there decides to move him again. I'm going to have proof this time, that he's dead."

"All right, but be fast and be careful of the door."

"Okay, I will be." He headed off towards the storage room.

Chapter Nineteen

After Jo texted Walt to meet her she walked towards the lobby. She could hear the questioning being conducted for the murder mystery. One voice was quite familiar.

"Sir Duncan, you claim that you were in the spa during the time of the murder, but upon review with the staff members that operate the spa, they insist that the spa was closed for repairs at that time. So dear sir, how could you have been in the spa if it was closed?"

"All right, All right, I wasn't in the spa."

The crowd gasped. Sir Duncan, played by Jeremiah, began to pace back and forth.

"Tell us the truth, Sir Duncan. Where were you? Why did you lie?" Samantha asked.

"I cannot!" Sir Duncan turned his back on Samantha.

"Then you must be the killer!" One of the

231

women from the event planning committee waved her hand through the air. "I want to solve the murder! It was Sir Duncan!"

"No wait!" Samantha shook her head. "Give him a chance to defend himself. Sir Duncan?"

He turned back slowly to face the crowd. His face was etched with shame as he looked towards Samantha.

"You're right, madam, I was not in the spa. I was with Rosita." He looked towards the actress across the room. "I lied, because I didn't want my wife to find out."

"You slime!" Marsha, in the role of Mrs. Duncan, hissed at him. "You are disgusting."

"Perhaps he's not the disgusting one, Mrs. Duncan. Because you claimed that Rosita was with you at the time of the murder. Which leaves you as the only person without an alibi. I accuse you, Mrs. Duncan, of murdering your lover, Count Allistair," Samantha said.

"Your lover?" Sir Duncan gasped.

The entire crowd gasped as well. The host of the murder mystery stepped forward.

"An official accusation has been made. If the accusation is correct, then the game is over, if it is incorrect, the game will continue, however the accuser will be out of the game."

"Samantha!" Jo grabbed her hand. "We have to go."

"Wait, I just..."

"Now." Jo looked into her eyes.

"Okay. Let's go."

As the host continued to ramble on about the rules of the game, Samantha, and Jo, walked towards the door. As they opened the door Samantha heard the host congratulating her on winning the murder mystery. She wanted to celebrate, but she knew that had to wait, Jo had something important to tell her.

As they walked towards the dining hall, they passed Walt in the lobby on the way and signaled for him to join them.

"I found the body." Jo announced as she turned to face them both. "It's in a freezer in the storage room. Eddy's gone to take pictures for evidence."

"Finally!" Samantha sighed with relief.

"But that doesn't tell us who killed Howard." Walt frowned. "Were there any clues in the freezer?"

"I don't think so. Well, his body was covered in a bedspread."

"Hmm, that's interesting. Maybe it was Howard's, or maybe it was the murderer's. If it wasn't the bedspread from his room that was used, then maybe we can figure out whose it was," Walt said.

"How can we do that? There are hundreds of rooms here." Samantha shook her head.

"I've been in close contact with the housekeeping staff since I arrived here." Walt smiled. "They told me that part of their bedbug prevention consists of putting the sheets and bedspreads through high heat before returning them to the beds. So they don't have them just stored in the closets. If someone used their bedspread, and then needed to replace it, they would have had to request a new one from the staff, and the staff keep strict records of what comes in and goes out so they can ensure that all of the bedding has been put through the heating process. It's actually a very impressive system."

"So we can find out who requested a new bedspread and that should at least tell us who moved the body?" Jo looked between the two of them. "It's our best lead so far."

"All right, I'll contact the staff, and find out who ordered new bedspreads." He glanced at his watch. "How long has Eddy been gone? Shouldn't he be back by now?"

"Yes, he should." Jo frowned. "I told him to be fast."

"We should go check on him. I want to see the body, too, maybe there's another clue that might have been missed." Samantha walked towards the door that led to the bar.

"I'll text you as soon as I hear anything from the staff. Let me know when you find Eddy please." Walt walked towards the laundry room.

When Samantha stepped through the door to the bar, she noticed Ben stocking the shelves.

"Afternoon ladies. Interested in a drink?" He smiled at them.

"No, thanks. Have you seen Eddy?"

"Eddy? No. Should I have?"

"He was on his way here about ten minutes ago."

"Oh, I might have missed him, I just got here a minute ago." He shrugged. One of the other barmen walked towards him.

"Baxter, we've got a problem with the ice blocks."

"What now?" Ben frowned.

"There aren't enough since the other freezer is

down."

"That's all right, we'll just have to make them last. Go out to delivery and see if the road is going to be clear in time to bring more tonight."

"All right, I'll be right back."

"Okay." Ben nodded and turned back to Jo and Samantha. "Like I said, I haven't seen him."

"Mind if we take a look in the back?" Jo locked eyes with him.

"Why would you need to look in the back?" He laughed. "Do you think Eddy was raiding the storage room for booze?"

"Certainly not." Samantha studied him. "He might have been looking back there for evidence, related to Howard's disappearance."

"Might have been? What do you think is back there?" He stepped around the bar and walked towards them.

"Baxter." Jo repeated the name. "I thought your name was Ben?"

"It is. Baxter is my last name. Most of the guys behind the bar call me that. All of the guests call me Ben, so it helps me figure out who is trying to get my attention."

"If it's no bother we'd really like to take a look. It's not like him to just disappear." Samantha's cell phone buzzed in her hand. She glanced down at the text that Walt sent.

The only request came from Ben's room. The bartender.

Her stomach twisted as she looked up from the phone to Ben, who paused right in front of both of them.

"What are you two up to?" He grinned as he looked between them. "I can tell, you're being sneaky."

"Oh no, we're just looking for Eddy so we can celebrate." Samantha shrugged.

"Celebrate?"

"Yes, I won the murder mystery."

"Oh? I didn't think they announced the winner yet."

"Just a few minutes ago."

"I guess I missed it. I've been in here stocking for a little while."

"I thought you said you just got here?" Jo crossed her arms. Samantha nudged Jo's foot with her own. Jo glanced over at her.

"We should go. Eddy's probably back up in his room by now." Samantha grabbed Jo's hand. "Let's go, Jo."

"What? Are you sure?" Jo looked from Samantha to Ben.

"That's probably a good idea. There will be a pre-dinner rush soon. Unless you ladies would like to stay, and have a drink? On me?"

"No thanks." Samantha tugged harder at Jo's hand. "We have to go."

"In such a rush." Ben cleared his throat. "It makes me think you really are being sneaky." He strode past them and closed the door to the bar, then he slid the lock shut.

"What are you doing?" Jo scowled.

"It's him, Jo." Samantha pulled her towards the door that led to the storage room. When she tried to open it, she found that it was already locked. Ben turned back to face them with a small, tight smile.

"You have caused me a lot of trouble. I had no intention of hurting anyone, other than Howard, but since you insist, I have no other choice. You can join your friend." He picked up an ice pick from behind the bar. Instantly, Jo wondered if that might have been the murder weapon. Eddy said it was a long tool. She could recall Ben using the ice pick to break apart blocks of ice for their drinks. She guessed there would be more than one of them.

"Just what are you planning on doing, Ben?" Jo stared at him.

"Come with me." He gestured to the door that

led to the storage room.

Samantha opened her mouth to scream, but Ben slammed the ice pick against the door right beside her head.

"Do you think you're still going to be alive by the time help comes? Hmm?" He glared into her eyes. Samantha closed her mouth and looked over at Jo. Jo shook her head just enough for Samantha to see.

"I'll be quiet."

"Good. Now, let's go." He pushed them ahead of him to the door. Once he unlocked it, he pushed them through it, then pulled the door closed behind them. As soon as Jo saw the freezer her stomach sank. She was certain that would be where her life ended. He jerked the door open to the freezer, then gestured for them to step in. "Let's go, inside."

"Ben Baxter." Jo stared at him. "Your father is Dan Baxter, isn't he?"

"He was." He locked his eyes to hers. "A long

time ago, he was."

"What do you mean?"

"I mean, because of Howard, I didn't have a father."

"You mean, you're his son?"

"No." He laughed. "I'd hate to be part of that gene pool. No, I'm not his son. I'm Dan Baxter's son. A man who could have lived a good life, who could have been a great father, but instead Howard wrapped him up in his lies and his cons, and he lost everything, even the will to live."

"What are you saying?" Jo tried to keep his attention. "Did something happen to your father? Did Howard hurt him?"

"Howard drained every bit of hope from my father. He took everything from him. He killed my father, even if my father was the one that pulled the trigger. Now get inside." He gave Jo a light shove.

"No." Samantha took a step back. "I'm not going in there."

"Yes, you are." Jo grabbed her hand and tugged her forward.

"Jo! No!" Samantha struggled to escape her grasp, but Jo tightened her grip.

"Sam, trust me." She looked into her friend's eyes.

"That's right, listen to Jo. She knows what's best." Ben shoved Samantha hard from behind until she stumbled into the freezer. She slipped on the icy floor and skidded across it until she slammed into something soft and cold.

"Ouch." With a grunt, Eddy opened his eyes.

"Eddy?" She straightened up and looked into his eyes. "Are you okay?"

"I'm freezing." He grabbed her and held her close to him. Jo rushed over to both of them and wrapped her arms around them as the door to the freezer swung shut.

"What are we going to do?" Samantha moaned. "This is it, we're never going to get out of here."

"Sh, I need to think." Jo rubbed her hands along Eddy's arms as Samantha stroked his cheeks and neck.

"Have you been in here this whole time?"

"Yes. Someone sneaked up behind me and shoved me in here. I didn't even get to see his face."

"It's Ben, the bartender." Samantha shook her head. "I never would have guessed."

"He's the son of Howard's business partner, the one who he opened the car lot with."

"Ouch, they lost everything." Eddy's voice trembled with the cold.

"From the sound of it, Dan Baxter lost a lot more." Samantha rubbed her hands together.

"There has to be a way out of here." Jo rushed up to the freezer door. They weren't dressed for the cold, and Samantha's body already trembled from the temperature change.

"Why didn't you let me fight him, Jo?"

"Because he would have killed you, Sam. You didn't see the look in his eyes. He's cold, very cold, and he doesn't care who he kills. I could see it in him. If you had fought him, you wouldn't have survived. At least this way we have a chance of escaping. Walt knows where we were going. He'll find us, I know he will."

"Right, and get shoved in here with the rest of us." Samantha shook her phone in her hand. "This thing isn't working."

"No reception." Eddy shivered. His lips had begun to turn blue.

"Eddy, are you sure you're okay?"

"I'm better than him." He tipped his head towards the body covered in the bedspread.

"Not funny, Eddy." Samantha nestled closer to him and tried to warm his exposed skin. Even though she was freezing, she knew he'd been in the freezer several minutes longer. "Please Walt, please find us."

"If anyone can, Walt can. Just try to stay

warm. Don't worry about me, Sam."

"I'm always worried about you, Eddy." She held him closer.

Jo wrapped her arms tighter around both of them.

"We just have to stay warm. Just for a little while."

Eddy's teeth chattered as he nodded. He wanted to be optimistic, but he wasn't. Walt might figure out where they were, but what were the chances that he would discover them in time?

Chapter Twenty

Walt waited eagerly for a text back from Samantha. He was sure that all of his friends would be impressed that he'd figured out who the killer was. After a few minutes passed with no text in return, he started to get anxious. They had been heading to the bar. What if Ben caught them? He hurried down towards the bar. All of the guests in the resort were gathered in the lobby and café, discussing the murder mystery. He picked up snippets of conversation.

"I can't believe she figured it out so fast."

"It would have been more fun if it lasted longer."

"Next time, we leave the detectives at home."

Walt did his best to ignore the comments and headed through the dining hall to the bar. As he approached the door, he heard something slam against it. His heart lurched and he froze where he stood. He thought about calling out for Jo and

Samantha, but his instincts told him not to. If Samantha hadn't texted him back, then it was very likely she was in trouble. He tried the knob on the door, but found that it was locked. He recalled that there was another entrance to the bar, through the kitchen, and through the storage room. As quietly as he could, he opened the door off the dining hall that led into the kitchen. Once he was through it he remained very still. He could hear voices.

"Jo! No!" He recognized the panic in Samantha's voice, and was sure that something terrible had happened. He heard Ben's voice next, then the sound of a heavy door closing. After a few minutes he heard Ben's footsteps as he walked away. He waited another full minute to be sure that Ben was actually gone. Then he rushed in the direction he believed the voices came from. It was the storage area of the kitchen. There were multiple closets, and boxes piled all over. It took him a few seconds to realize that the door he heard close, was the door to the freezer. He grabbed the handle and tugged. No matter how hard he pulled he couldn't get the door to open.

"Samantha! Jo!" He pounded on the door. "Are you in there?"

He heard something that sounded like muffled voices from inside. His panic increased as he knew they wouldn't survive long in the cold temperature. He looked for something to pry the door open with, but couldn't find anything. He needed help. Without time to consider other options he dialed Bart's number.

"Bart! It's Walt. Jo and Samantha are stuck in a freezer in the kitchen! I need security, I need help, I can't get the door open."

"We're on our way, Walt." Bart hung up the phone. Walt wasn't sure if he would come. Jo had been very suspicious of him. What if he decided to take his time to send help? He had to figure out how to get the door open himself. Again, Walt pulled at the door. He couldn't understand why it wouldn't open. It shouldn't have been locked.

Then he saw it. Ben had wedged a piece of metal in the hinge of the freezer to prevent it from opening. He kicked it hard until it was free. Just as he swung the door open to the freezer, Bart and two security guards arrived in the kitchen.

"Walt? Walt! Where are they?" Bart's voice carried through the kitchen storage area.

"Back here!" Walt peered into the freezer. "Jo? Samantha? Are you in there?"

"We're here." Samantha helped Eddy to his feet and tried to push him ahead of her.

"I can't, I can hardly move." Eddy shuddered.

"It's okay, just keep trying, Eddy, we need to get you out of here."

"I've got you, Eddy." Jo grabbed his cold hand and pulled him forward. The more Eddy moved the more flexible his body became. He stumbled out of the freezer and fell into Walt's arms.

"Yikes Eddy, you're ice cold." Walt struggled to support his weight.

"Get a medic down here, now!" Bart barked into his radio.

"It's Ben, the bartender." Jo shuddered and rubbed her arms. "He's the one that killed Howard, and put Howard's body in the freezer."

"Ben?" Bart swallowed hard. "I'll be sure to find him."

"He put us in the freezer just a few minutes ago, he can't be far." Samantha narrowed her eyes. "He was going to kill all of us."

"Ben wouldn't do that." Bart cleared his throat. "I'll find him!" He ran out of the room as the medical staff arrived to evaluate Eddy. After a few minutes and some warm towels, Eddy was finally able to feel his body again.

"Wow, that was close. I wasn't sure if anyone would come looking for me in time."

"Too close." Samantha shook her head. "I had no idea Ben was behind all of this."

"I'm sorry, I never put the two last names together." Walt's shoulders slumped. "If I had maybe you never would have been in danger."

"Walt, it's not your fault. You're the only one that figured it out. Did you ever find out who Howard's son is?"

"It's Jeremiah. I was able to find a record of his birth and confirmed it."

"Do you think maybe they worked together?" Samantha shivered and pulled the blanket that the medical staff gave her, tighter around her shoulders. "Maybe Ben and Jeremiah decided to get rid of Howard."

"I don't know, but I don't think Ben worked alone." Jo pursed her lips.

"What do you mean?" Eddy looked over at her.

"I'm not sure yet. Let's go make sure that Ben gets arrested."

"There's something happening in the lobby." Walt poked his head out into the hallway. "Maybe they've got him."

When they reached the lobby they found Bart, with Ben in his grasp, and two other security guards around him.

"You're not going anywhere, Ben. It's done, the police are on their way." Bart shook his head.

"Fine, I don't care. Howard got what he deserved, and that's all that matters."

A few of the actors and actresses as well as some onlookers gathered around the group.

"Why?" Jeremiah called out from the crowd. "Why did you kill him? You didn't have any right!"

"Because, he killed my father first. Howard was his business partner, and he conned him and gambled all of the money away. My dad lost the business, the house, everything, all because of that drunk, greedy fool. So yes, I killed him. He deserved to die. He was worthless, and I decided to do the world a favor. When he told me who he was, I asked him how he could even look me in the eye. You know what he told me?" He stared hard at Jeremiah. "He said that he was sorry, and he had some money that he wanted to split between you and me. That's why he'd come back to the resort. He wanted to split it between us. I told him, I didn't want his money. I didn't want anything to do with him. Nothing could bring my father back. He demanded that I listen to him. That I take his money, because he wanted to start over, he wanted to have a relationship with his son. When he said that, I just, I lost it." Ben shook his head and lowered his eyes. "I will never get that relationship with my father, because of him. Why should he get to have one with you?" He looked up at Jeremiah again and glared. "I thought with his ex-wife, and the loan sharks, and the guy from the casino being at the resort, I had a good chance of getting away with it."

"You were wrong." Eddy scowled at him. "Murdering him was terrible."

"It was nothing compared to what he did to my family. People can't just get away with that!"

"That's not it though, is it?" Jo turned to face Bart.

"What do you mean? We found the body, we found the killer, the murder is solved."

"The murder, yes. But Ben wouldn't have been able to pull all of this off, not with your eyes constantly on the resort."

"I don't know what you mean." He frowned.

"Earlier, when I found the body, you said you saw me go into the bar on the camera. But the camera was pointed away from the door of the bar. I noticed it when I went inside. So why would you lie? You clearly didn't see me on the camera."

"Uh, well, it must have been one of the other cameras as you headed for the bar."

"There's no camera in the dining hall. All you could have seen was me walking down the hallway outside of it. So are you going to tell me that you were able to figure out exactly where I was based on that?" She gestured to the two men beside him. "Don't let him get to his gun."

"Stop, this is nonsense. I did nothing wrong." Bart sighed. He held up his hands as the two

255

security officers turned towards him. "Put your hands on me, and you're going to lose your jobs."

"Why don't you tell the truth, Bart?" Eddy glared at him. "From the start you didn't want to admit that I saw a body. You kept insisting that I might have been confused, or drunk. Ben's admitted he was the killer, but I'm certain that he didn't do it on his own. I'm betting when the police do a full investigation of this, they're going to agree with me. It's better if you admit it now."

"Okay, look, I didn't kill Howard. I didn't have anything to do with that."

"No, you just wanted to protect the resort." Jo rolled her eyes. "Money is more important than human life."

"No, that's not it either. I wanted to protect Ben." He looked over at the man in handcuffs. "He's not a bad person. He really isn't. He just snapped. When he first came here, he was a mess. He had no one to look out for him. I made sure he got a job, and got himself stable. Not many people can survive what he did."

"His father's bankruptcy, and his suicide." Eddy nodded. "Yes, that must have been hard on him."

"He looked at Howard like he was his hero. He had no idea who he was. But I did. I research everyone that gets hired here. I knew that Ben was Dan's son. I knew that Howard was responsible for Dan's death, but I didn't think it would be a problem if Ben never found out. I knew that Howard inherited the money and he said that he planned to tell Ben the truth. I told Howard to leave things as they were, but I was worried that he wouldn't listen to me. That's why I told Callie to contact Howard's wife, and why I tipped off Carlisle and Billings. So they all knew that Howard was back. I even told Billings about the inheritance. I figured one of them would be able to take care of my problem, get rid of Howard, and Ben could keep living his life in peace. But it didn't work out that way. I was too late and Howard decided he wanted to make amends straight away, and so he confessed who he was to Ben."

"He actually asked me to forgive him." Ben growled. "Why should he get to have a relationship with his son when he took my father from me? Why should he get to clean up his act and be a better man while my dad is cold in a grave because of his schemes and addictions?"

"It wasn't his fault." Jeremiah crossed his arms. "He didn't put the gun in your father's hands."

"No, he just stripped a good man of every ounce of his worth. My mother left him, and he thought he had nothing left to live for."

"I'm sorry that happened to you, Ben. Growing up without a father, I know what that's like. But it didn't give you the right to commit murder. When Howard told me who he was, I couldn't believe it. I was so angry. I told him that he'd ruined everything, that he didn't deserve to be alive, and I meant it in that moment. My mother struggled so hard on her own, and he never even cared. But he really was trying. At least, I thought he was." Jeremiah lowered his eyes. "I guess I'll never know now."

"I'm sorry, Jeremiah. I wouldn't wish this kind of pain on anyone, but it was worth it. Howard had to pay. My father can finally rest in peace."

"You saw Ben moving the body, on the cameras, didn't you, Bart?" Jo looked back at him.

"Yes, I did. I saw him. There wasn't time to think about it. I just knew we had to hide the body as fast as we could. I thought, Howard would have killed himself eventually, he would have ended up dead somewhere in a drunken stupor."

"Except, he did stop drinking." Jeremiah frowned. "Who knows how long it would have lasted, but maybe he could have turned his life around."

"You're just as guilty, Bart." Eddy nodded to the security guards beside him. "Cuff him."

Bart didn't struggle as the men beside him

secured the handcuffs around his wrists. Instead he looked right at Jo.

"I thought maybe you would understand."

"Not murder, no I will never understand that."

Outside the lobby there was a roar of an engine. Samantha looked over to see a large snowplow clearing the driveway that led to the front door. Behind the plow were several police vehicles. The blizzard had come to an end, and so had their real life murder mystery. Yet, she was no longer quite as excited about the cruise she'd won. Eddy wrapped an arm around her shoulders and pulled her close.

"You did good, kid."

"Then why doesn't it feel that way?" She tilted her head to the side to look into his eyes.

"Because a man is dead, and there's no way to feel good about that. But thanks to us, his son knows the truth, and his killer will pay the price. That's the best that we can do."

"I guess that's good." Samantha frowned.

"We did our best, Sam. It's a very good thing." Jo patted her shoulder.

"Yes, I guess it is." She sighed. "I think this was the last activity I'm going to plan for Sage Gardens. Clearly it didn't work out well."

"I wouldn't say that." Walt smiled. "You solved two mysteries in one weekend. That's pretty great if you ask me."

"Samantha!" Amber waved to her from a small group of women gathered near the café. "Do you have a minute?"

"Here it comes." Samantha grimaced and slipped out from under Eddy's arm. As she walked over to the women, Jo stepped up beside her.

"We just wanted to tell you that this was the most amazing trip." Amber smiled. "All of this drama and intrigue, it was better than watching a movie, it was like being part of it."

"I guess I can see that." Samantha nodded and managed a smile. "I'm glad you enjoyed yourselves."

"We've decided you should be in charge of all of the activities." Amber looked at the other women, then smiled at Samantha. "You handled the crisis like none of us could have, and still made sure we had a fun weekend."

"Wow? Really?" She braced herself for the laughter. Surely they had to be joking.

"Really." Amber nodded. "Thanks for all of your hard work."

"Thank you." Samantha smiled. For the first time she felt welcomed by the women who she'd been trying to connect with since she had moved to Sage Gardens.

"Come with us, let's have some tea." Amber turned towards the café.

"Jo?" Samantha looked over at her.

"You go ahead, I'm going to take a walk in the snow." Jo smiled.

"Do you want company?"

"I think you're occupied." Jo laughed.

"No. I'm not. Thanks ladies, I'll catch up with you when the bus loads up." She linked her arm through Jo's. "Let's go freeze our buns off together."

"Wonderful. Did I ever tell you about the time that I went sledding in shorts and a bra?"

"What?" Samantha laughed as they walked away from the café. It was nice to feel included, but it was even better to know that she could rely on Jo's friendship. As the two waded out into the snow, they were joined by Walt and Eddy.

"Did you know that frostbite can begin to affect your skin in only..."

"Walt!" Samantha and Jo laughed.

"What? It's very important information."

"Yes it is, pal, yes it is." Eddy threw a snowball straight at him.

"Don't, it's full of dirt and smog and..."

"Ouch, better get that snow off your nose,

Walt, you don't want to get frostbite." Jo laughed and wipe his skin clean with her hand.

"Ugh." He sighed and looked into her eyes. "Thanks."

"Don't worry, I'll avenge you." She scooped up a pile of snow and formed it into a tight snowball before hurling it at Eddy. Their snowball fight continued until all four were too cold to play anymore. That night they sat by the fire in the lobby and listened to memories of Howard shared by the staff and the actors. In the middle of their conversation Walt slipped away. When he returned some time later, he took Jeremiah aside, and gestured for his friends to join him.

"What is it?" Jeremiah looked between them. "I don't think I can take anymore shocks."

"Your father recently received an inheritance."

"And?" Jeremiah frowned.

"And we had no idea where it might be. There's no record of it being in any account. But I do know he planned to give it to you," Walt said. "I also knew that if he had it in cash, he had to have it nearby. So I looked through his room. It didn't take me too long to find the loose floorboard in his room. The money is there now along with a note explaining why he wanted you to have it. The police have already searched his room and didn't find it."

"But what about all of his debts?"

"They were his debts, not yours, Jeremiah. You were the only one willing to give him a second chance. I can't tell you that he would have sobered up, or that you might have had a relationship, but I can tell you that he cared enough to try to make amends, and that's something. So let him."

"Thanks, I will." Jeremiah offered them a small smile. "Thanks for everything."

By the next morning the parking lot was clear and the bus was ready to take them back to Sage Gardens. Samantha made sure that everyone was on board, then waved goodbye to some of the staff members as she climbed on the bus as well.

Walt settled into his seat with perfect posture. Eddy put his headphones on to drown out the impending singing. Jo opened one of the books she borrowed from Eddy, and Samantha sat down with a sense of gratitude for her friends. As the resort disappeared behind them, Samantha gazed at the large glass windows that sparkled with the reflection of the sun off the surface of the snow. It was a beautiful place, which now had its own tragic story. Maybe if they hadn't been there, Howard would have remained a missing person forever. At least now his son knew that his father didn't just disappear for a second time, and his killer knew that revenge wasn't as sweet as he expected. The only question that lingered on her mind, was what kind of mystery would be waiting for them when they got back to Sage Gardens.

The End

More Cozy Mysteries by Cindy Bell

Sage Gardens Cozy Mysteries

Birthdays Can Be Deadly

Money Can Be Deadly

Trust Can Be Deadly

Ties Can Be Deadly

Rocks Can Be Deadly

Jewelry Can Be Deadly

Numbers Can Be Deadly

Memories Can Be Deadly

Paintings Can Be Deadly

Chocolate Centered Cozy Mysteries

The Sweet Smell of Murder

A Deadly Delicious Delivery

A Bitter Sweet Murder

A Treacherous Tasty Trail

Luscious Pastry at a Lethal Party

Trouble and Treats

Dune House Cozy Mysteries

Seaside Secrets

Boats and Bad Guys

Treasured History

Hidden Hideaways

Dodgy Dealings

Suspects and Surprises

Heavenly Highland Inn Cozy Mysteries

Murdering the Roses

Dead in the Daisies

Killing the Carnations

Drowning the Daffodils

Suffocating the Sunflowers

Books, Bullets and Blooms

A Deadly Serious Gardening Contest

A Bridal Bouquet and a Body

Bekki the Beautician Cozy Mysteries

Hairspray and Homicide

A Dyed Blonde and a Dead Body

Mascara and Murder

Pageant and Poison

Conditioner and a Corpse

Mistletoe, Makeup and Murder

Hairpin, Hair Dryer and Homicide

Blush, a Bride and a Body

Shampoo and a Stiff

Cosmetics, a Cruise and a Killer

Lipstick, a Long Iron and Lifeless

Camping, Concealer and Criminals

Treated and Dyed

Wendy the Wedding Planner Cozy Mysteries

Matrimony, Money and Murder

Chefs, Ceremonies and Crimes

Knives and Nuptials

Mice, Marriage and Murder

Macaron Patisserie Cozy Mysteries

Sifting for Suspects

Recipes and Revenge

Nuts about Nuts Cozy Mysteries

A Tough Case to Crack